"Beautifully written, with a concert-hall perfect pitch for adolescent speech and idiom and ways of feeling."

— Charles Baxter, National Book Award finalist

"The final score in any game is always clear; Patrick Hueller's engrossing novel Kirsten Howard's Biggest Fan captures the messiness of life that hides behind those numbers."

—Carl Deuker, bestselling author of *Gym Candy* and *Swagger*

"Hueller has written a powerful story about family trauma and deep friendship that sings with a love of sport and hope. What a joy to read."

—Geoff Herbach, award-winning author of *Stupid Fast* and *Hooper*

Kirsten Howard's
BIGGEST FAN

By Patrick Hueller

INtense Publications
www.intensepublications.com

INtense Publications
Paperback ISBN: 978-1-947796-36-2
Kirsten Howard's Biggest Fan
Copyright © 2020 Patrick Hueller

This is a work of fiction. Names, characters, places and incidents are either the product of the author's imagination or are used fictitiously and any resemblance to actual persons, living or dead, business establishments, events or locales is entirely coincidental.

This edition published by arrangement with INtense Publications LLC. The opinions expressed by the author are not necessarily those of INtense Publications LLC.

www.INtensePublications.com

To every teenager who spent their childhood playing pickup, reading Matt Christopher or Mike Lupica or Walter Dean Myers or the next day's boxscores, watching football on the weekends and playing it with neighborhood friends during halftime, and arguing about the rules of a sport you and your friends modified or completely made up.

FALL SEASON

WHEN KIRSTEN HOWARD, STAR basketball player for the Rapid River Raiders, showed up at my front door, she didn't knock.

She would have, I'm sure, but I didn't give her the chance.

My best friend Eric Pendleton had just texted me—*where r u? The service is almost starting*—and I opened the door while yelling over my shoulder to my parents: "Off to church with Eric. Be back later!"

When I turned my head, there she was: standing in a Minnesota Timberwolves basketball jersey, holding the screen door open with one arm, a basketball under the other. The two of us stood there awhile, neither of us saying anything. In Kirsten's defense, for some reason, she was trying to catch her breath.

In my defense, Kirsten had turned hot.

Sweat poured down her arms, streams of it collecting at her elbows before dripping on the concrete next to her sneakers. Strands of her hair were plastered to her forehead. She smelled a little like a locker room.

But she was all of a sudden so hot I didn't know what to do with myself. I was aware of my hands and couldn't decide where to put them.

Don't get me wrong, I'd been in love with Kirsten since I first saw her dribbling circles around the other girls way back in elementary school. But it was never a romantic thing.

I just loved the way she dribbled.

Somewhere between the spring and this moment, though, Kirsten had changed. I'm in tenth grade, she's in ninth, which means 1. we go to different schools (me: high school, her: junior high), and 2. I hadn't seen her in months. In that time, she'd done some serious growing—an inch or two in height, but that's not the kind of growth I'm talking about.

Kirsten had grown breasts.

Nice ones.

Her basketball jersey, one I'd seen on her before, was now a little snug.

And it wasn't just her chest. It was *all* of her. Even stuff that couldn't possibly have changed seemed different. Her light brown hair was pulled back in a ponytail, except for those few strands that must've dislodged on her way here. The too-little tooth poking out next to her front teeth. Even those sweaty-drippy elbows.

All there before. All somehow different.

Kirsten broke the silence.

"You're going to church in those clothes?"

I looked down at my t-shirt and wind pants and tugged at the brim of my baseball cap. "No. I mean, not really. It's sort of a joke. An inside joke."

"Oh," Kirsten said, looking puzzled.

"It's a long story," I added. "Did you run here from your house?" I mean, duh. Obviously, that's what she'd done. "Isn't it hard to run while carrying a basketball?"

She shrugged her shoulders. "I didn't carry the basketball. I dribbled it."

From her house? That was like three miles—most of it along a *highway*.

Turns out Kirsten was kind of crazy.

And completely awesome.

Kirsten still looked confused. "Is Coach around?"

"Coach?"

"Coach Duncan? A.k.a. your father?"

Oh. Right. She was clearly here to see my dad, *the head coach of her basketball team*. She may have been only a freshman, but she'd been starting—and starring—on the varsity team since she was in seventh grade. Had I actually thought she was here to see me?

"Yeah," I said. "Yeah, he's downstairs."

"Great." Kirsten jerked her head at the ball under her arm. "Thought I'd talk with him about the upcoming season."

"Cool. I can go get him if you want."

"That's okay." She took a step toward me and then around me, squeezing by my shoulder. "You're in a hurry. Do I just go down the hall?"

"Yeah," I said, "but—"

I was about to tell her that she wasn't really allowed to go down there, that no one was, that for a couple of hours a day Dad could be found in the basement, with the lights off, *studying*. That was his word for it, and it meant that he was watching a film of whatever Rapid River sport he was currently coaching (football in the fall, basketball in the winter). He didn't hang a *Do Not Disturb* sign from the door handle during these study sessions, but that's only because he didn't have to. Mom and I knew the rules.

I didn't get to tell her any of this, though, because she was already moving down the hall, her ponytail bouncing behind her.

When she got to the end of the hall, she turned around and pointed to her right. "This door?"

"Yeah, but—"

"Thanks, Mike." She grabbed the door handle, looked at me one more time, and said, "You look really different, you know? Seriously, I hardly recognized you."

"You, too," I started to say, but she had already opened the door and headed downstairs. She must have been skipping or something because I could hear every footstep as it hit the stairs. I waited a few minutes for her to come back up again. *Sorry*, I'd tell her, *I tried to warn you*. But she didn't come back up, and after a while, my phone buzzed again.

It was Eric: *u r gonna miss the sermon.*

I typed back that I was on my way.

"SO KIRSTEN CALLED YOU Mike," Eric said. He tossed the wiffle ball back to me. "What's the big deal?"

"She's never called me that before." I leaned in and squinted as though I was getting hand signs from an invisible catcher.

We were in his backyard, playing one-on-one wiffle ball. Or, as we liked to put it, we were attending church.

The Church of Baseball.

Eric took his hand from the wiffle bat to ask an imaginary umpire for time. He stepped out of an imaginary batter's box. "Last time I checked, Mike is your name," he said. "Mike Duncan—unless you had it legally changed and didn't tell me."

Actually, if we're getting technical, my name is Michael Jordan Duncan. Say it fast enough, and it sounds like Michael Jordan *Dunking*. Which, believe it or not, was intentional. My dad didn't just name me after a sports player; he named me after a sports *play*. How he slipped this past my mother I'll likely never know. It was a sore subject between them.

Eric stepped back into the batter's box and I threw him a pitch. He whiffed.

"She usually says Michael," I said.

"Mike, Michael." Eric chucked the ball back to me. "What's the difference?"

"Mike sounds way more personal. Especially with the other stuff she said."

Eric took a few practice swings. "She said you looked different. What's so good about different?"

"She meant tall."

Like Kirsten, I did a lot of growing over the summer. Unlike Kirsten, my growth had been entirely vertical rather than horizontal.

"And that's supposed to be a compliment?" Eric said. "Randy Johnson's six-foot-eleven and he was like the ugliest pitcher in baseball history."

He took another practice swing, then tapped the fingers of his left hand on his chest. He was making the sign of the cross like former major leaguer Ivan Rodriguez used to do before every pitch.

There were actually two Churches of Baseball. One was Eric's backyard, where we took turns hitting wiffle balls and pretending we were famous hitters and catchers; the other was the high school baseball field. On Sundays during the summer, when Dad wasn't too busy with coaching, he would bring Eric and me to the high school and hit us grounders and fly balls for a couple of hours, then take us to Big Scoop, our local ice cream shop. Dad came up with the name. My mom asked where we were headed and Dad, wearing cleats and holding a bag full of baseballs, said, "Church. Where else?"

After that, the name stuck.

"I guess *Walter* Johnson was pretty tall and wasn't *that* ugly," Eric said. He stepped up to the tree root we use as home plate. "So maybe she doesn't think you're *completely* hideous."

I was pretty sure Walter Johnson was a pitcher a long time ago. Did I mention Eric is a genius freak when it comes to baseball trivia? Most home runs? Most strikeouts? Most nut cup readjustments in a single at-bat? Eric could not only provide the answers but probably the exact number.

I threw him another pitch, a curveball. He whiffed again. Strike three.

As much as he *knows* about baseball, though, he's always been terrible at playing it. No matter how often we practiced or how many tips from current or former players he dug up, he never seemed to get any better. I don't know why; there's nothing physically wrong with him. He's scrawny enough that he swims a little in his clothes, but you wouldn't look at him and think weakling. In fact, if you were a new kid at school, you might even assume he was a good athlete. You'd look at the baseball jerseys he always wore and see his perpetual hat hair, and you'd think he was some sort of jock right up until he was the last guy picked in gym class.

"So what's next?" Eric said as we switched places. He became the pitcher; I became the batter. "You two get it on until she finds someone even taller?"

"Funny," I said.

Eric threw me a pitch and I, doing my best impression of Hall of Famer Ken Griffey Jr., took a swing, letting go of the bat with my left hand a split-second after making contact with the wiffle ball. The ball flew across the yard and over a wooden gate into his mom's garden. I only realized she was in the garden when the ball came sailing back over the fence along with her voice.

"Aren't you boys a little old for this?" she said.

"Sorry, Mrs. Pendleton," I said.

"Sorry, Mom," Eric said.

Eric and I grinned at each other. Mrs. Pendleton had been telling us we're too old for wiffle ball for years.

"Reconvene next Sunday?"

"Of course." I flipped the plastic bat in my hand so I held the barrel.

Eric took the bat and said, "Kirsten going to your game on Friday?"

I hadn't thought of that.

"Let's hope not," I said.

THAT FALL WAS MY first time playing football.

My growth spurt got me on the field. Before that, my mom wouldn't let me play because she thought I was going to get killed. But over the spring and summer I grew nine inches—from 5'1" to 5'10", and Mom finally caved. "Fine, Michael," she said. "If you want to break your neck, be my guest."

Because this was my first time playing, you'd think I spent most games standing on the sidelines, right? That's what *I* thought I'd be doing.

But I was wrong.

I was one of two *starting* wide receivers, and I played the majority of the game.

It took me a while to figure out how this was possible. Was it because my dad was an assistant coach on the varsity team? Or because I tried so hard in practice? Or because I had natural-born talent at catching footballs?

No, no, and no.

I was a starting wide receiver for one reason and one reason only: no one else wanted to do it. I was on the JV team, but I might as well have been on the junior high squad. Maybe then our team would have stood a chance. Even if our quarterback, Patrick Kent, had a good enough arm to throw it to the receivers—he didn't—our undersized offensive line couldn't block long enough for him to get the throw off.

I may have been a starting wide receiver, but I hadn't had a single pass thrown my way all year.

It was the last game of the season, and—as usual—our team was losing. Big. For some reason, Coach Lind called a timeout late in the fourth quarter and shuffled his way from the sideline to our huddle. We were all bent over, breathing hard, wondering what was up.

When you're down 42-6 with only a minute and forty-eight seconds to go, what's the point of calling a timeout?

"Jesus," Elliot Balstad said. "Can't we just get this game over with?"

"Don't worry," Andrew Ness said. "Coach has a 60-point play up his sleeve. I feel sorry for the other team. They probably think they're going to win."

Players laughed wheezily as Coach arrived.

At first, he didn't say anything. He just looked at us, his eyes going from one helmet to another.

When they got to me they stopped.

"This play is for Duncan," he said.

It was so surprising, I blurted, "To me, Coach?"

"To you, Duncan. That okay with you?"

I almost asked *why me?* but stopped myself just in

time. "Sure," I told him. "I mean, yeah, absolutely."

Coach explained the play and then told us to bring our hands to the middle of the huddle. We all said, "Ready, break!" before going to our positions on the field. As I trotted out to the right, I was pretty sure one of my teammates pounded my shoulder pad, but I couldn't be certain. I was so nervous, my whole body had gone numb.

I didn't know why Coach called this play, except that maybe he thought I was the last player the other team would expect to get the ball. Either that, or he figured we were losing 42-6, with only one-minute, forty-eight seconds to go, so why not try something crazy?

The play we were running was a double-wide-out reverse, which wasn't something we'd ever tried before. Coach actually had to draw it up on his hand so we understood what he wanted us to do.

And now here I was, standing way off to the right, telling my body to take it easy and not start running until the ball was snapped. My arms twitched and my hands felt cold and slippery.

I took one glance at the stands and saw that they were starting to fill up for the varsity game. Okay, *fill up* is an exaggeration. The varsity squad was almost as bad as we were, and it wasn't as if any fans had to worry about getting turned away at the ticket booth. I saw Eric up at the top of the bleachers, where he and I had been sitting every fall Friday since we were kids. For a split-second, I wondered if Mom or Dad were there watching, even though I knew better. Mom was still at work, and Dad was in the locker room with all the varsity players.

He wouldn't come out until they did, the players running in front of the coaches, stomping through the end zone and tearing through a big sheet of blue-and-gold-colored paper held by the cheerleaders.

I wondered if Kirsten was there, or if I wanted her to be.

I wasn't sure I wanted anyone to see this.

It was maybe six-thirty and it wasn't too dark yet, but the lights were coming on anyway, warming up for the big game. They felt as if they were all directed at me—every megawatt bulb adding to a spotlight shining on me and me alone.

The ball was snapped, and I tried not to look left too soon and give the play away.

When I did look, I saw that the play was already a bust.

All the defensive players had trampled our linemen and were charging after the quarterback, who just had time to pitch the ball to the wide receiver coming from the other side, John Atkinson, who caught the ball and started running toward me.

John was running for his life. He had what appeared to be their whole team chasing him, and he was bringing them to *me*.

And since I didn't know what else to do, and I was already moving in that direction, and fear had me on some sort of automatic pilot, I ran to the ball.

To John.

To the guys trying to get the ball and kill whoever had it.

Right before they pulverized John, he tossed me the

ball. I snatched it out of the air and took off running in the other direction.

I ran backward toward my own end zone, then horizontally toward the sideline, then, finally, up field, passing the line of scrimmage and heading in the direction of the other end zone, the *other team's* end zone, the *correct* end zone, though it was still a good fifty yards away.

There was no one ahead of me. Most of the other team was no doubt behind me, chasing me like they had been chasing John.

By now I'd been running for what seemed like forever—from one side of the field to the other, from one end to the other—and my chest was low on oxygen. I still had thirty yards to go, and it felt as though I'd been holding my breath for minutes. My lungs felt exactly like they did when Eric and I used to go to the local pool as kids and see who could swim underwater the longest.

As I ran with the football, I told myself to keep going, to keep it up, to pump my arms and push harder and make it, make it, make it. The end zone got bigger and bigger—only ten yards to go.

Make it. Make it and you can come up for air.

That's when a player appeared in my periphery. He was only a few feet away, and he dove head-first for my legs. His helmet slammed into my knee.

And then I felt and saw nothing, nothing but pain.

And I heard a giant *Pop*

I SPENT THE NIGHT on the living room couch because I couldn't make it up the stairs to my room. The next morning, I tried to concentrate on a *Sports Illustrated* article on Chris Paul. But reading about basketball just made my knee feel worse.

"Mind if I watch some of the pre-game shows?" my dad said.

I told him I didn't. We stayed like that for a while—me on the couch, Dad on the chair next to it—watching the ESPN commentators evaluate which teams had the best shot to win that week. That Dad was watching ESPN on a Saturday wasn't surprising. He spent most fall Saturdays watching college football. What was unusual was that he was watching TV this early. Usually, he'd be downstairs studying last night's film until almost noon.

During a commercial, Dad said, "Think I'll go ahead and make some of my special waffles—the ones with the secret ingredient. Want one?"

I shook my head. I was in no mood for breakfast.

Besides, Dad's "special waffles" were just the frozen kind you put in a toaster. His "secret ingredient" wasn't much of a secret, either: all he did was put a chocolate chip in each little square.

Still, his offer was pretty significant. Dad hadn't made me breakfast since before the season started, and I knew he was just trying to be nice.

Dad nodded. "In that case, you want to tell me about the prognosis?" He gestured toward my knee.

I wasn't in the mood to do that, either. "Didn't Mom already tell you?"

Dad shook his head. "When she found out I wasn't the one who took you to the hospital, your mother wasn't exactly pleased. I thought it best to keep a wide berth."

He tilted his head toward the basement door.

As sorry for myself as I felt at that moment, I couldn't help feeling sorry for him, too. "You slept downstairs?"

He had done this before, but only when Mom was really pissed.

"So what did the doctor say?" he asked.

I told him. A grade three sprain. The meniscus. Two-month recovery time.

"No surgery?" he asked.

I shook my head.

"That's good news."

I wasn't so optimistic. "That's what the doctor said. But two months means I won't be able to play basketball until Christmas, Dad. And that's if I'm even allowed on the team. And why would I be?" Suddenly I was talking very quickly. "The whole point of tryouts is to cut people.

If I'm not at tryouts, I'm just making the coach's job easier. What is he going to do? Cut an extra player so I have a spot once I've healed?"

Now that I was done airing my grievances, I heard my mother's footsteps come down the stairs. I hoped she hadn't caught my complaining, because I knew it would only make things worse for Dad.

I watched him watch her enter the living room. "Mike was just filling me in on the injury," he told her. "What a bummer."

Mom stood somewhere behind the couch. I still couldn't see her. "If you had taken Mike to the hospital, he wouldn't need to fill you in," she said.

"That's true, Mary," Dad said, "he wouldn't." But he sighed in a way that made it sound as though he didn't really agree with her. Then he got up, walked past her, and headed for the basement.

It's not like Mom never used the basement. The washer and dryer were down there, and so was an elliptical exercise machine. But as far as I knew, that day was the first time Mom ever *followed* Dad downstairs. That's how angry she was.

Even then, she didn't go all the way into the basement. I knew because she didn't shut the door all the way. When I sat up and craned my neck I could see her standing toward the bottom of the stairs, but still on the stairs, which technically wasn't *in* the basement, just on the stairs that *lead* to the basement.

Then a strange thing happened. As I looked at Mom, an image of Kirsten Howard inserted itself into my view: there she was, ball under her arm, skipping down the stairs, brushing Mom's shoulders as she breezed on by.

"Explain to me how this isn't choosing sports over your family, Jeff," Mom said, and just like that Kirsten vanished. "I'm totally willing to listen. Just take me through the thought process that results in this not being you caring more about sports than your son."

I hated seeing Mom like this—hands on her hips, lips pursed, standing rigid—so I lay down again.

Truthfully, I felt bad for both of them. This was just a newer, angrier version of the argument they always had. Mom didn't live and breathe sports, which meant for her they would always just be games. If a father chooses to coach a game instead of taking his son to the hospital, he's clearly choosing sports over his family. Even if somebody else volunteers to drive the son to the hospital, as John Atkinson's father did. And even if the son *tells* the father that he should stay and coach, as I definitely did.

The thing is, for those of us who love sports, this love doesn't seem like a choice at all. That sounds crazy to a lot of people—and maybe it is. But it doesn't *feel* crazy. For a sports nut, making sports a top priority feels like common sense. It feels like second nature.

"I don't care," I heard Mom say. "That's not good enough, Jeff."

I tried to tune her out because the sports vs. family argument was ongoing and totally hopeless. Mom and Dad would yell for a while and then give each other the silent treatment until the argument didn't seem like such a big deal anymore. I think I was in third grade the first time I remember watching them have this fight.

Dad had taken me to a girls' high school basketball game between Lakeshore and Groveland. Before the game, he showed me how to keep a shot chart. I was still holding the shot chart when I got home, and Mom freaked out. She told dad that he was a liar—that he tricked her—that he didn't go to the game to be a good father; he went to be a good scout. I remember being shocked. As far as I was concerned, he had been a *great* father. He'd taught me how to keep a shot chart and then trusted me to do it right. Until Mom started yelling, I'd felt like Dad's assistant coach.

Finally, Mom came back upstairs and asked me if I wanted eggs or pancakes for breakfast.

I said, "Cereal is fine."

"Oh, come on," she said. "Really, I don't mind." And unlike Dad, who listened to me when I said I wasn't hungry, Mom went to make eggs or pancakes, or both, even though I just told her I didn't want them, and somehow that made me feel even more hopeless.

A few hours later, Dad came upstairs. "I just talked with Andy on the phone," he said to me.

"Andy?"

"Andy Wight. Your JV basketball coach."

He looked at me but spoke loudly enough for Mom to hear.

"I used to scout with him before I took the job as the girls' coach," Dad said. "I think you'll really enjoy playing for him."

I sat up. "Wait. Does that mean I'm on the team?"

Dad smiled. "How much you do or don't get to play, that's going to be up to you and Andy. But he says he'll save a spot for you on the roster."

Now I smiled, too. "Thanks, Dad."

He didn't say anything, just nodded and turned and headed downstairs again, pulling the door closed behind him.

I looked into the kitchen at Mom. She hovered by the counter, using an electric mixer, and I wondered if she'd even heard Dad over the noise.

IT WAS STRANGE. EVEN though I wasn't mad at Dad for staying at the game while I went to the hospital, I *was* mad at Eric.

Dad had a game to coach. He wasn't the head coach, but he was the offensive coordinator, which meant he called all the plays when Rapid River had the ball. Besides, I *told* Dad not to worry about me.

But Eric? What was his excuse? He didn't even like football—not compared to baseball or even basketball—but he hadn't stopped by once to check on me. Not before I went to the hospital, not at the hospital, not since I had gotten back from the hospital.

I didn't realize how mad I was until Eric texted me Sunday morning.

Church? the text said. *Where r u?*

I was still lying on the couch as I read the message, and I almost told him that.

On the couch gasping my last breath, I typed.

But I erased that text and tried for something

simpler.

What do u care?

Then I erased that, too, and decided to just forget it. If he wanted to talk to me, he knew where I lived.

Not too long after that, someone knocked at the door. At first, I thought it was Eric, but then realized it couldn't be. He would have just come in. We've been to each other's houses so often since elementary school, our parents finally instructed us not to worry about knocking.

Mom answered the door. "Oh, hi," I heard her say. "Did you come to see Michael? Come on in."

After a few moments, John Atkinson came into the living room. He was wearing adult clothes—a collared shirt, a tie, a vest—all of which made him look younger, not older. He had long hair in front that he usually let hang over his eyebrows but today had combed to the side.

"Hey, man," he said.

"Hey."

His head drooped a little, not quite looking at me. "My parents," he tilted his head to indicate they were outside, "they thought—I mean, I thought—you know, that I should stop by and see how you're doing."

I didn't know what to say. His parents brought him to visit me? I felt embarrassed for both of us.

"Thanks," I said finally. "I'm fine."

"Cool," he said. "Okay, well, I better get going to church."

"Sounds good."

He turned to go, but then turned back. For the first time, he looked at me. "Damn, Mike," he said. "When did you get so fast?"

He said the words quietly, as though the question and my answer were somehow confidential.

"What?" I said.

"You were *flying* down that field. You have turbojets on your ankles or something?"

He leaned in, waiting for my response.

"Oh. Thanks," was all I could think to say.

John stood upright again. "Take my word for it," he said. "You've got some serious wheels."

By the time I said thanks again he was heading for the door. He probably didn't even hear me.

Which was fine—because I didn't hear me, either.

I was too busy replaying what he had just said to me. *Turbojets, serious wheels*—I cranked up his voice several decibels so every word was loud and clear.

The words weren't loud enough to drown out Eric's entrance, though. He must have entered the house just as John exited it because I heard John say, "Hey, Eric," and Eric says, "What are *you* doing here?" John told him nothing, that he was just leaving, and I listened to Eric squeak down the hall.

His cleats, I thought. Eric was wearing his cleats again.

One of the main differences between our two houses was the rule on footwear. His parents didn't care about shoes being worn inside; mine did.

Both of us sometimes forgot the other house's rules

on footwear. The result was Eric marking up our floors (I swear, my mom had a super-heightened vision when it came to finding marks—her eyes detected them like how a black light detects bodily fluids on hotel beds), and I snagged my socks on nails that stuck out of the Pendleton's' old wood floors.

My mom was upstairs, and just knowing she was there made the squeaking seem louder than it probably was.

At least they're plastic cleats, I thought.

"Hey," Eric said as soon as he spotted me on the couch, "what was Buttbreath doing in your house?"

Something I forgot to mention about Eric: for various reasons, he didn't get along with the other guys at our school, especially the athletes. His hate for them ran deep enough that he had given most of them nicknames beginning with the word Butt: Buttmunch, Buttfat, Buttsweat, etc. Collectively, he called them the Butt Clan. He'd been doing this since like seventh grade, but I could never remember who was called what.

Usually I didn't mind him calling these guys those things. It was pretty funny. They were my sports teammates, and none of them had ever done anything to me personally—but several of them had treated Eric like crap over the years, which was Eric's explanation for calling them Butt-something-or-other.

This time, though, the name bugged me. To my knowledge, John had never personally mistreated Eric—not to mention the fact that he'd come to see me before my so-called best friend did.

"He has a name," I said.

"I know. It's Buttbreath," Eric said. He stood at the end of the couch, right where John stood a few minutes ago. He had his backpack on but was wearing his baseball glove. I wondered why he didn't just put it in the backpack. "You were skipping church to fraternize with the enemy?"

"I wasn't fraterni—"

"What happened to you?" Eric interrupted. His eyes, suddenly big, were on my knee.

"What do you mean, *what happened to me*?" I said.

"What do you mean, *what do you mean*?"

This conversation, clearly, was going nowhere.

"The leg," Eric said. "Why is your knee the size of a softball?"

"What are you talking about? You were *there*."

"I was there…"

"At the game. When this happened. I *saw* you."

Eric contemplated this. He rocked forward and backward, his cleats digging into the carpet. "Yeah, but I didn't see you," he said. He sounded apologetic.

"What the hell does that mean?"

"It means I wasn't watching, Mike. Sorry."

"You weren't watching… when? I was on the ground for a long time."

"I wasn't watching *ever*," he said.

I didn't get it.

"Sorry, Mike. It's just, you know, you don't ever get the ball, and…." He let his words trail off. He stared at my leg again.

"And?" I said.

"And that's why you didn't show up for church this morning, huh?"

I didn't bother to say yes. "You want to tell me what you *were* doing?"

More contemplating, more rocking.

"Reading."

Reading? At a football game? Who reads anything other than a program at a football game?

"Must've been a good book," I said because I couldn't think of anything else to say.

Eric nodded. "Not just a good book, Mike, a great book. The greatest book."

I started to say, "What are you talking about?" but Eric was already taking off his backpack. He got in a catcher's crouch, unzipped the backpack, and pulled out a huge hardcover book. "What's that?" I said.

"The Bible, Mike. *Our* Bible."

He walked it over and held it up for me to look at. The cover was brownish-orange and had a coffee-mug stain on it. I read the title of the book out loud: "*The Baseball Encyclopedia.*"

"This book, Mike.... *This* book right here...." As Eric tried to finish his sentence, his voice raised from hushed awe to something more excited. "Every player or statistic you could ever want—it's all right here in this book.

"Wow," I said. It *was* impressive. "Where'd you get it?"

"My relatives in California sent it to me. Found it at a garage sale or something." Eric clutched the book to his chest. Then he held the book out and smiled. "How's this for service? If you can't make it to church, I'll bring the sermon to you."

He opened the book and asked me to pick a ballplayer, any ballplayer.

I SKIPPED SCHOOL ON MONDAY.

It was Mom's idea, not mine. I spent the night on the couch again and woke up to Mom and Dad talking about me in the kitchen. I couldn't see them, but judging by the sound of their voices, Dad was only a few feet away from me at the kitchen table, and Mom was farther away, by the sink and cupboards.

"The doctor said he could go back as soon as he felt up to it," Dad said.

"I know, Jeff," Mom said. "I was there, remember?" I heard the whine of a cabinet door being opened.

"So you don't think he's up to it?"

"I'm just worried about all the stairs," Mom said. "He hasn't even made it up to his bedroom."

Dad's chair slid backward. "Fine by me," he said. The faucet turned on. "Should we wake him up and ask him what he thinks about—"

"Fine by me," I blurted out.

It's not that I hate school—I like it for the most

part—but I'm not crazy. If you have the chance to miss school, it's practically your duty as a student to take it.

I spent the day napping and watching ESPN. At some point, I muted the TV and described the sports highlights myself. *Maybe if this knee never heals*, I thought, *I can have a future in sports casting.*

As I described a long touchdown pass— "Down the sideline . . . stride for stride . . . arms outstretched . . ."— I heard a bouncing sound.

It came from outside.

For the first time that day, I got up for some reason other than getting food or going to the bathroom. I locked my crutches under my arms and moved around the couch and down the hall. Through the front door window, I saw what was making the noise.

I saw *who* was making the noise.

Kirsten Howard.

She had on a different jersey this time: Lebron's gold Cleveland Cavaliers jersey. She dribbled hard to the hoop but had enough body control to ease up at the last moment, seemingly mid-air, and make the layup.

Kirsten kept at it: dribbling and shooting with her right hand on the right side, dribbling and shooting with her left on the left side. Her center of gravity remained low. Her shoes screeched. It looked gray and cool outside, but her arms gleamed with sweat.

I could just make out the freckles on her shoulders.

After a while she switched to reverse layups, taking

off on the opposite foot of the hand she shot with.

I considered going out there and asking what she was doing here. Besides the fact that this wasn't her house, Rapid River Junior High didn't get out for another half hour or so. I got as far as placing my hand on the door handle when I chickened out. She looked so intense, I didn't want to interrupt. If she made it clear she didn't want to talk to me, it wasn't as if I'd be able to claim I was just passing through—not on these crutches.

Maybe, I thought, *I could say I was getting the mail.*

Except I wasn't sure whether the mail had come yet. Even if it had, how, given the crutches, was I going to carry it? In my mouth? In the elastic waistband of my shorts?

Besides, I hadn't showered in three days.

No, going out there would be a bad idea—as would continuing to stand there, looking through the window. What if she saw me? *Oh, hey, Kirsten. Don't mind me. I'm just staring at you—feel free to keep doing what you're doing.*

Instead, I went upstairs.

Two crutches and one step at a time, I made my way to the landing and then started up the second half of the staircase. The desk in my room faced the window, which faced the driveway, and I leaned over it and watched Kirsten move from layups to five-foot jump shots. She put enough backspin on her shots that most of them bounced right back to her after they went in. When they didn't—go in or bounce back to her—she hustled after them so the ball didn't get too far away.

She kept shooting from five feet until she'd made

twenty or so in a row from every spot possible, then backed up to seven or eight feet and followed the same procedure.

It was at this point that Eric came strolling down the driveway.

No, strolling isn't the right word. Waddling is more like it.

He wore not one but two backpacks—one in back, one in front. Kirsten spotted him after I did. She rebounded her shot and turned his way. They said something to each other, and then Eric looked over her shoulder and right at me—which caused Kirsten to start to turn her head, and me to dive to the floor.

Which wasn't a good idea.

Technically, it wasn't an idea at all. I didn't consciously think about what I was doing or make any sort of decision. My instincts—*don't let Kirsten see you ogling her*—did my decision making for me.

In any case, it hurt. Howling pain hurt. Except I couldn't howl, because I wasn't sure how sound-proof my window was.

A few minutes later, Eric found me on the floor, sitting up, the howling pain beginning to quiet down.

"Hey, Mike," he said. "You all right?"

"Yeah," I said. "What are you smiling about?"

"Nothing. Brought your school books."

He let the backpack in front slide off his arms and land next to me on the floor.

"Oh," I said. "Thanks."

"No problem."

"What the hell are you grinning at?" I repeated.

"Relax, Mike. She didn't see you. I mean, she knows you're in here somewhere—what was I supposed to tell her? —but I don't think she saw you spying on her like some perv."

I didn't know what to say to that.

"Your secret's safe with me," Eric said. Then he turned around to leave.

"Where are you going?"

"I've gotta run."

"Where?"

"To do research. I was looking through the Bible today and found something potentially really interesting." He slapped the backpack he still had on to indicate the location of "the Bible," aka *The Baseball Encyclopedia.*

"What?"

"Not sure yet. That's why I have to do more research."

Eric Pendleton, tenth-grade scholar. "You're practically hyperventilating," I said.

"That's because this thing, it could be *big*," he said. "But I have to be certain of my findings before I announce them to the world at large."

"The world, meaning..."

"Just you, I guess." Eric slapped his backpack again. "I'll let you know more when I know more."

"Deal." He headed for the door. "Hey, Eric?"

"Yeah?"

"Tell her you found me watching TV or something—

you know, something completely un-stalker-y."

"You got it. I'll say, and I quote, 'Don't worry, Kirsten. I found him doing something completely un-stalker-y.'"

He left.

I sat there, back to my desk, for a few more minutes. Out of the corner of my eye, I saw the mini, fake-leather basketball under my bed. I've had the ball since I was in elementary school. Cotton stuffing stuck out of one of the seams. Leaning over and grabbing the ball, I imagined Kirsten still out there shooting and stared at the plastic rim that's bolted to the wall across the room.

If I make this, I told myself, *Kirsten Howard digs me.*

Still sitting, I took a shot and watched the ball bounce off the rim, off the wall, and under the bed again.

I sat there a few minutes longer, then reached for the ball again.

That was just a warm-up, I thought. *Now for the real shot.*

I DECIDED I WANTED to skip school the next day too.

As Mom sat down at the dinner table, I made my case.

"Eric brought all my books home today," I told her, "so I can miss tomorrow and still stay caught up on my homework."

Mom said, "Sounds like a good discussion for the whole family." Usually I'd be optimistic about this response. I was reasonably certain Dad would say the same thing he said that morning— "Fine by me"—and then it would be up to Mom to make the final decision. But for reasons I wasn't going to explain to her, this time I wanted her to make her decision *before* Dad came upstairs.

I was about to continue to plead my case when Mom got up, opened the door, and said, "Jeff—dinner's ready."

Dad hollered back, "Thanks, Mary. Be there in a minute."

Mom closed the door and sat down again. "It's not

like your father to be late for the family feast."

The last part, about this being a feast, was Mom's sarcastic way of making fun of her own cooking. When I was six, I gave her an apron for Mother's Day, and ever since she's worn it right over her business clothes; the apron says *Chef Mom* in green puff paint, the words surrounded by several green circles with green dots in them that were meant to be either pepperoni pizzas or chocolate chip cookies. Mom liked to point to the apron and say, "Chef Mary's my name and cooking's my game."

Mom's a businesswoman, a consultant or something, and every once in a while, when she was held up at a meeting, Dad would step in and make omelets or a frozen pizza. When I was younger she was actually gone quite a bit—she'd go to two- or three-day conferences in other states—but then she changed her position in the company so she could be around more. Most days of the week she prepared the meal, especially during football and basketball season. After having been at work all day, she usually didn't have much time to make something fancy, so in an effort to "streamline the operation" (her words, not mine), she'd come up with a daily dinner schedule. Sundays we had chicken and instant rice, Mondays we had tacos, Tuesdays we had stir fry and instant rice, etc., etc. (We had a lot of instant rice.) Anytime Dad or I would try to compliment the food, Mom would say something like, "What can I say? I slaved away for hours." Then she'd go to the pantry, grab a box of Oreos and say, "I even made dessert."

This time, though, her comment about it not being

like Dad to be late for the family feast wasn't just a joke. The part about Dad was true. If he wasn't at a game, Dad usually set the table.

"Plus," I said, getting back to my skipping-school request before Mom's patience ran out completely, "today I tried going up to my room and I fell. It hurt really bad."

This wasn't a lie, I told myself. I *had* gone up to my room, and I *had* fallen. The two events weren't related, of course, but I didn't technically say they were. Putting them in the same sentence isn't the same as saying one caused the other.

Mom stood up and partially rotated to untie her apron and set it on the counter behind her. "Since when do we wear hats at the table?" she said.

I didn't answer. The reason for the baseball cap was that I knew something she didn't.

It wasn't just Dad in the basement.

Kirsten was down there, too.

She'd continued shooting until Dad got home from football practice. Then the two of them went downstairs to study film from last year. I was still in my room at the time, but I heard them enter the house. Dad said something like, "I noticed this last weekend after you left, and I've been meaning to point it out to you . . ." Then I'd heard the door to the basement open and close.

They were already down there when Mom got home and started getting ready for dinner. I didn't tell her about Kirsten because by then I'd decided that I wanted to skip school again and didn't want to put her in a bad mood before asking. All these years of steering clear of the basement, and now Dad granted access to one of his players? There was no way Mom was going to like this.

So instead of mentioning Kirsten, I helped Mom set the table. I got the plates and glasses and silverware out. I folded the napkins. I dumped some shredded cheese in a bowl and put it on the table. I had the baseball cap on during all of this—there was no way I was letting Kirsten see three days' worth of dirty hair—and Mom was in a good enough mood that she didn't tell me to take it off. Or maybe she just assumed I'd take it off once dinner started. It was nothing new for Dad or me to be wearing a hat when we got back from a practice or a game, so maybe Mom thought I planned to get rid of it once we started eating.

"I don't have any major homework or tests tomorrow," I reassured her, "so I'll be able to make up whatever I—"

Just then the door opened, and Dad came through, and Mom looked at her watch and said, "I guess my reputation as a chef preceded me. For a second there I thought you were boycotting my tacos."

Kirsten stepped out from behind the door just as Mom finished her sentence.

"Hey, Mrs. Duncan," Kirsten said. "Hey, Mike."

I nodded and touched the bill of my cap, then felt like an idiot because only old people greet someone by touching the bill of their cap. Next, I'd be calling her "Ma'am."

"Sorry to make you wait for dinner," Kirsten said. "Coach Duncan was showing me some stuff to work on before the season."

Mom didn't say anything.

"I hope I didn't ruin the food," Kirsten said.

Mom still didn't say anything.

"You're fine," Dad said. "Do you want to stay for dinner? Mary makes a mean taco."

"Oh, thanks," Kirsten said, "but I better not. Mom will kill me if I miss dinner. I'm probably late already."

To my surprise, Mom said, "Jeff, you can give her a ride, right? That way she won't be late for *her* family's dinner."

Kirsten said thanks but no thanks. "Really, Mrs. Duncan. It's fine."

Mom insisted, though: "You shouldn't keep your family waiting."

So Kirsten said, "Thanks, Mrs. Duncan," and "Seeya, Mike," and she and Dad turned to go.

Mom and I listened to the garage door open and close. Then she went to the oven and removed the pan of taco shells. She brought the pan over to me and said, "Dig in."

As I reached for a shell, she said, "If you want to stay home tomorrow, stay home tomorrow. I'm sure your father doesn't care one way or the other."

Then she grabbed my cap off my head and threw it like a Frisbee through the kitchen and over the living room couch.

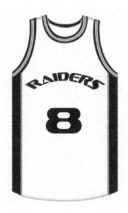

IN CASE IT'S NOT CLEAR already, the reason I asked to stay home for a second consecutive day had nothing to do with my knee.

It had nothing to do with pain or with going up or downstairs.

It didn't have anything to do with skipping class, either. As I said, I like school. I like sitting down in my desk knowing that by the time I get up again I'll have brand new information in my brain. If you think of it like that, school becomes kind of like the movie *The Matrix*. Not like the matrix itself—I'm not saying school is a conspiracy to cover up the fact that the world is actually run by aliens and computers—but like those chairs the characters sit in to learn how to do kung fu or fly a helicopter. In the movie, this information is literally injected into characters' heads (like a flash drive into a computer), and I imagine the same sort of thing happening whenever I sit down at my desk.

So yeah: I liked school.

Just not as much as I liked Kirsten Howard.

As I sat on my floor in my room the day before, it occurred to me that her showing up to shoot on my driveway might not be a one-time deal. For one thing, Kirsten brought her backpack with her. If she had been home from school for some reason (sickness, family emergency, some religious holiday I wasn't aware of, etc.), she would have left the backpack at her house, right? As far as I could remember, she'd never worn the backpack any of the previous times she'd dribbled to our house.

Plus, when I glimpsed out the window again I realized the basketball she was using wasn't hers. The ball she usually brought was a rubber one. This one was leather. In other words, it was an indoor ball, not an outdoor one. And when I looked closer, I was pretty sure I saw some letters scrawled on it with marker, which was true of all the equipment owned by either the junior high or high school.

All of this proved that she'd left from school, not home—even if it didn't explain how or why.

So I thought there was a good chance she'd come the next day after (during?!) school, too, if only because of the *way* she was shooting. When people are just shooting for the hell of it, just messing around, they take shots from wherever the ball bounces before they grab it. They take their time. They might try some trick shots, or chuck up a few three-pointers, or pretend they're going for the game-winning shot.

Kirsten hadn't done any of that.

Instead of taking her time, she hustled after the ball and then to a specific spot on the court/driveway. And there was nothing random about her shot selection: she started close to the basket and moved out gradually. No trick shots. No threes. No leaning, off-balance, game-winning jumpers.

Her shooting was methodical. It was routine.

It was *a* routine.

Which meant she followed the same shot pattern over and over again. And that she would follow the same routine the next day, and the next day after that.

Probably.

Maybe.

Hopefully.

Anyway, there was only one way to find out.

At 2:30 in the afternoon, I was both disappointed and relieved that Kirsten hadn't shown up.

At 2:36, I was both relieved and disappointed that Kirsten showed up. As always, she dribbled as she charged up the driveway.

I'd had all day to get ready for her appearance but I suddenly felt totally unprepared. I went over the plan again—what I had come up with to do and say—and it seemed both lame and poorly thought-out.

There was a hitch in my plans that somehow hadn't occurred to me. Earlier, I'd imagined casually crutching my way to Kirsten and then casually asking, "Wanna rebounder?" Then, if and when she said yes, I'd casually offer the girls' basketball I was holding. (Girls' basketballs are slightly smaller than guys' basketballs. We had one, I guess because my dad's a girls' basketball coach. But that doesn't mean we ever used it. When I'd found it in a bin in our garage, I discovered it had gone flat, so I pumped it up.) Unlike the leather, indoor basketball Kirsten was using, this one was meant to be used outdoors. According to my plan, Kirsten would accept my casual offer and I'd casually pass her the ball. But as I stood at the front door, I realized that being casual was going to be impossible. How do you do casual when you've got two crutches, one basketball, and only two arms? Was the ball supposed to just materialize— abracadabra! —when I needed it? I'd kicked the ball from the garage, through the entryway, down the hall, and to the couch in the living room, but had somehow managed not to consider that moving the ball would be just as difficult later on.

And now it was later on; later on was right now. I stood on the front steps, a crutch under each arm. I propped the front door open with my rear end as I used one of the crutches to drag the basketball through the door.

It was totally awkward, and my only thought was, "Please don't let Kirsten see this. Please, please don't let her see thi—"

"Mike?"

I swiveled my neck and found Kirsten staring at me.

"Hey," I said.

"Hey. Need some help?"

The basketball rested at my feet and she nodded at it.

"No," I said. "Think I got it." Then I said, "Thought maybe you could use this, so you don't scuff up the indoor ball."

In my head, when I imagined making the offer, it had

sounded helpful—but out loud it sounded like I was scolding her: *how dare you ruin a perfectly good basketball*. The fact that I knew she was using an indoor basketball also meant I must have been watching her really closely. Which I had been. But still. I didn't want her to know that.

"Thanks," she said.

If she thought my comment sounded weird, she wasn't acting like it.

"Ms. Mattson gave me this one," she said. "She was in the middle of explaining the rules of some game to a bunch of seventh graders and I interrupted class to ask for a ball. She went into the equipment room and before she even came out this ball was rolling at me. From like thirty feet away. She must have had to hook her arm around the door frame to get the right angle. By the time I picked it up and saw it was the wrong kind of ball, she was already talking to the seventh graders again."

Kirsten paused, breathing hard—either from all the shooting or from talking so fast. She gulped some air.

"I almost interrupted class again to tell her," she said, "but I chickened out."

"Oh," I said. Because I didn't know what else to say.

And then, all of a sudden, I wasn't quite so nervous—mainly, I think, because Kirsten obviously *was* nervous. Or maybe she was embarrassed. The point of her story, I realized, the reason she started talking so fast, was that she wanted me to know that she knew the difference between an indoor and outdoor ball. She was in a hurry to prove to me that she would never intentionally use the wrong ball—which meant she cared what I thought about her, at least when it came to discussions regarding basketballs.

Which was pretty cool.

"The thing you have to remember about Ms. Mattson is that she's quick as a cat," I said.

Kirsten laughed. Ms. Mattson had to be at least sixty-five years old. "Oh, yeah?"

"Don't let her ancient brittle bones fool you," I said. "That woman's stealthy."

Kirsten laughed again.

Of all the ways I had pictured this conversation going, I had never imagined making her laugh. Not intentionally. Not *with* me instead of *at* me.

"Well," I said, "here comes another basketball rolling your way." Instead of kicking it, I hit it to her with one of my crutches. I even considered getting down on the ground and using my crutch like a pool cue. That's how loose I suddenly felt.

Kirsten scooped the ball up with one hand and discarded the other one on the lawn next to the driveway. She had a baggier jersey on today, and when she twisted at the waist to watch the indoor ball come to a rest, I could see some of her sports bra under her arm. She looked back at me and took a couple of dribbles.

"Thanks," she said.

"Don't mention it," I said.

When she didn't say anything else, and I didn't say anything else, and the two of us had been standing facing each other for what felt to me an awkward amount of time, I turned to go back inside. Better to quit while I was ahead, I decided.

But then Kirsten said, "I'm sorry about the knee."

I pivoted on my good leg to face her again. "Yeah. Looks like I'm going to miss some of the basketball season."

"That's what Coach Duncan said."

Coach Duncan equaled my dad. No matter how many times she said it, I still had to do the equation in my head.

"The team is saving a spot for me, though—for when I get back."

"That's cool," she said.

She didn't seem as impressed with the news as I was, and I wondered if that was because Dad already told her this, too, or because she'd never had to worry about a spot being reserved for her. If she got hurt, Dad would hold out hope until the last day of the season that she could come back. And for good reason. Without her, the season would be pretty much over. She was that good.

"What are you doing here, anyway?" I asked. "I mean, why aren't you at school?"

"Coach Duncan rigged it. I have study hall last period, and Coach and I were talking, and he offered to write a whole bunch of passes to get me out of school so I could get my shooting in."

"Sounds like my dad," I said.

He was always up to something. Sometimes it was like he didn't think the rules and expectations of others applied to him. Usually, he ended up being right. In Dad's first year as head coach, he and the girls did lots of fundraising and got new uniforms, and then he surprised everyone by giving away all the old ones to senior girls who weren't on the team. *For free.* By that time, the varsity practice uniforms had already been passed down to the lower grades to be used as game jerseys, which meant Dad had to fundraise *again* for new practice uniforms. At first, this didn't go over too well. People grumbled about it being a waste of money, and it wasn't until the first home game that people started to come around. All the girls who'd been given the old uniforms came running onto the court with the actual team, and then, when the team sat down on the bench, the girls in the old uniforms sat in the rows right behind them. This meant that the JV and varsity squads sat in the first row, the sophomore team sat in the second, and the girls in the old uniforms sat in the third, fourth, and fifth rows. Back then, girls' basketball wasn't at all popular—Dad could barely get enough girls to fill a roster, let alone fill the stands. But to the opposing team, it looked as though Rapid River had five rows' worth of screaming, cheering players. At the end of each season, he had the senior fans pass their jerseys on to junior girls in order to keep the tradition going.

Right from the beginning, Dad had explained his plan to me. I knew parents wouldn't like paying for new jerseys because Dad told me they wouldn't. I knew that he was going to give the jerseys to other players, and that he'd have them sit in the bleachers, and that their uniforms would give the girls on the bench a new sense of team pride. I knew that parents and fans would instantly forget about having to pay for more jerseys when Rapid River won the game (which they did). Everybody that day—players and fans alike—were on their feet cheering as the buzzer sounded. I can still remember Dad finding me in the bleachers and holding up his hands as if to say, "What'd I tell you?"

So, yeah—Dad was always pulling strings. To my knowledge, though, this was the first time he'd helped someone skip school.

"Why do you come here to do it?" I asked Kirsten. "I mean, isn't your house closer to the school?"

Kirsten lived in town. We lived just outside it.

"Yeah," Kirsten said, "but our driveway isn't as flat or wide as yours. And anyway, it's a good excuse to work on my dribbling."

I couldn't help laughing. The location of our house did seem to Kirsten like a good excuse to practice her dribbling, even though for most people it probably seemed like a good excuse *not* to dribble, or run, or even walk. There was no bike path or trail of any kind—just a shoulder and a metal railing. It was hard to imagine anyone not named Kirsten Howard choosing to travel along the shoulder of a highway with or without a basketball.

"What's so funny?" Kirsten said.

"Forget it," I said. Then I said, "Want someone to rebound your shots?"

THE NEXT DAY I went back to school.

After fourth period, a guy named Jake Nichols waited for me in the hallway. He was leaning against the far wall, and when he saw me he straightened and took a few steps in my direction.

"Can I help you with your bag?" he asked me.

"I think I can manage."

"Cool." Jake walked alongside me as I crutched down the hallway toward the cafeteria.

This was an unprecedented event in my life—Jake Nichols walking in the hall with me—and I didn't know what to make of it.

Jake and I grew up playing basketball together, but we didn't really know each other. For one thing, our b-ball careers had gone a lot differently. Jake had his growth spurt young, which meant he was a star for most of elementary school and was one of the most popular guys in school. In fifth grade he was already 5'7" or 5'8", but he hadn't grown more than an inch since. His playing time decreased, but his popularity hadn't.

His giant head of big curly hair wobbled as he walked. I still hadn't gotten used to looking down at kids who had always been way bigger than me.

"You probably already know this, man, but you were positively *hauling* at the game on Friday. I had no idea you could chug like that."

I was pretty sure *hauling* and *chugging* were good things, so I said thanks and then added, "It was fun while it lasted."

He tilted his hair toward my braced knee. "Yeah— tough break, man. It's gonna heal though, right?"

"So they tell me," I said.

We passed the library and the main office and entered another hallway. At the end of the hallway was the cafeteria. Jake walked alongside me as I crutched to the front of the cafeteria for the hot lunch line.

After I got in line and headed for the trays it occurred to me I had a problem. How was I supposed to carry a tray and my crutches at the same time? (Why I don't see these problems coming from a mile away, I honestly can't tell you. My face should probably be permanently fastened to my palm.) Jake must have seen me hesitating or staring too long because he grabbed two trays instead of one.

"I got this," he said.

"Thanks."

"No one should go hungry on Italian Dunker Day," he said.

"Best day of the week," I agreed. It was almost a good enough reason to be at school, even if it meant missing out on Kirsten's arrival on my driveway.

Almost.

Once we were out of the line, Jake said, "You wanna sit with us today?"

Us.

As in, Jake and all his popular friends.

As in, the table I'd never sat at, even though it was where most of my teammates ate lunch every day.

I followed Jake's gaze to the table. John Atkinson thumb warred with Nikki Paulsen while holding a sandwich in the other hand. Nikki laughed and squirmed in her seat as she tried to pull her thumb out from under John's.

I almost said, "Can Eric sit with us?"

But then, right on cue, I heard his voice: "Give it back, Buttcrust!"

I turned in time to see Adam Pilsner entering the cafeteria. Eric was right behind him—or right in front of him since Adam was backpedaling. Eric practically stood on Adam's shoelaces. Adam held Eric's *Baseball Encyclopedia* high in the air. "Take it easy, Pendy," he said. "I just wanna check this thing out."

Eric, I knew, wasn't listening. Not anymore. He was so angry and desperate he had likely forgotten where he was. His mouth moved very fast and I knew he was muttering a constant stream of swear words just loud enough for Adam to hear.

I knew this because I'd seen it before. Lots of times. Eric could always be counted on for two things: sports statistics and spazzing out. He'd been interested in the first category since elementary school and had been guilty of the second for just as long.

Eric and I had talked about this a lot—about how he was always egging people on—and he agreed that he wasn't helping himself out. But for some reason, he couldn't stop.

Couldn't stop the eruption of anger that burned his face and spewed out of his mouth. Couldn't stop ridiculing Adam or whoever else was bugging him... until the bugging escalated into torture.

Worst of all, he couldn't stop the tears from leaking out of his eyes.

Simply put, Eric Pendleton was a crier. My best friend since forever was a gigantic crybaby. Always had been, maybe always would be. Most kids stop crying regularly in public around third grade, but not Eric. It wasn't just bullying that caused it, either. In junior high, he bawled over bad grades, a bad play on the sports field, or just bad luck.

Over the years it had gotten a little better, I think, but not much.

Which meant that it had gotten worse.

If you want to commit social suicide, become a high school guy who sobs openly in the halls of your high school.

Adam stopped at the front of the cafeteria, by the trash cans about twenty feet to my right, and continued to hold the book in the air as Eric jumped up and down for it. I knew it was only a matter of time before Eric's voice cracked along with whatever puny dam held back the flood of water from his eyes.

The tears were coming. There was no question that

they were coming.

I wasn't even watching Adam anymore. Or listening to what either of them said. I just stared at Eric, at the corner of one of his eyes, and thought: *Hold them in, Eric. Hold them in.*

Luckily, Adam took mercy on him this time—or, more likely, he simply got impatient. Instead of taunting Eric with the book until the waterworks flowed, he tossed it in the trash and sauntered over to the cool table.

As he passed me, he patted Jake on the top of his curly hair and said, "Dunker Day. Score." Then he said, "See you at the table, Jakers" and kept moving to his table.

By the time I looked for Eric, he had his head and shoulders buried in the trash bin.

That was when I realized I hadn't answered Jake yet.

"Thanks," I told him. "But I better sit over there."

Jake told me to suit myself and followed me to my usual seat. He set the tray down and said, "Maybe some other time. Later, man."

"Later," I repeated.

I set my crutches on the linoleum floor and tried to think of something other than how my best friend was currently doing a face plant into a trash bin.

A few moments later, Eric sat across from me at the lunch table. Rather than the trash can, he buried his head in his backpack. He pulled out a notebook and slid it around the backpack in my direction.

"Mikey," he said, "good to have you back." The top of his hat was all I could see of him behind the backpack. It moved a little as he talked. Eric wore a baseball cap every second of every day. I mean that almost literally. When we were younger and had sleepovers, he'd undress inside his sleeping bag—take off his pants and socks—but he'd keep his hat on. The only time he didn't wear a baseball cap was when someone, usually a teacher, told him he had to take it off.

Or when some other kid took it off to play keep-away, just as Adam did with The Baseball Encyclopedia.

"How's the leg?" Eric said. Honestly, judging by his voice, it was as if other than my leg there was nothing wrong in the world. His eyes, which were almost for sure red around the edges, were hidden behind his backpack. If I hadn't seen Adam take the Encyclopedia, I would have never suspected that there had just been an incident.

That's another thing that was weird about Eric. He could be publicly humiliated and, once it was over, instantly forget that the humiliation ever occurred. In a sense, I suppose that was a good thing. It would be really hard—on Eric and everyone else around him—if he couldn't get past getting picked on. He got bullied enough that hanging out with him would be non-stop depressing.

This ability to forget embarrassment was also annoying, though. He might have been unconcerned with the social damage that had just taken place, but I wasn't. It was bad enough that there were still kids looking at him and laughing, but the fact that they were laughing in my direction too made it even worse. What's that word for it again? When you're killed or hurt because you're standing next to the actual target? Collateral damage—that's it. That's what Eric made me.

At least it's Dunker Day, I told myself.

Which was pretty much the only hot lunch at Rapid River that was edible. And which, I'm convinced, had the power to solve just about any problem. There's something deeply satisfying about the whole process of eating Italian dunkers. On their own, the ingredients are underwhelming: French bread that's either stale or hard from being defrosted; a slab of cheese that's either rubbery or plastic-y but definitely isn't cheesy; and a gob of sauce that's either too runny or too goopy on its best days. Put all these things together, though, and you have a delicious delicacy.

I peeled off the non-cheesy slab of cheese and felt my irritation peeling away, too.

Then I pressed down on the top of Eric's now-empty backpack until it deflated enough for me to see him. He was looking down at the *Encyclopedia*, which he had balanced between the edge of the table and his lap.

"What's this?" I asked, nodding toward the notebook.

"Remember when I told you I needed to do some more research?"

I picked at another slab of non-cheesy cheese. "Uh-huh."

"Well," he said, "I haven't completed the research,

but I've done enough to confirm my initial hypothesis."

"Oh, yeah?" What was this—science class?

"Open it," he instructed without looking up.

I did.

On the first page there was some sort of entry:

```
Name:    Walt Alston
Born:    1911 (Ohio)
Games:   1
At-Bats: 1
Hits:    0
Homeruns:  0
Stolen Bases: 0
Runs:    0
Batting Average:.000
```

"Who's Walt Alston?" I asked.

"Turn the page."

Another entry:

```
Name:    Tom Kirk
Born:    1927 (Iowa)
Games:   1
At-Bats: 1
Hits:    0
Homeruns:  0
Stolen Bases:  0
Runs:    0
Batting Average:  .000
```

Was this supposed to answer my question?

"Who are Walt Alston *and* Tom Kirk?" I asked.

"Ex-major league ballplayers," Eric said.

I looked at Tom Kirk's statistics again. Mostly zeros. "Just barely," I said.

"Pretty incredible, right?"

"I don't get it," I said.

Finally, he looked up. A bit of lettuce clung to his cheek. Garbage lettuce. From his nosedive into the trash can.

"Mikey—these players, they made it all the way to the big leagues and have, like, *nothing* to show for it. No home runs, no runs, not a single solitary hit."

"I can see that. So what?"

"So what? So they made it to the major leagues, made it into a game, and then never played again."

"Oh, gotcha," I said, even though I didn't. "Hey, I think you've got something on your cheek."

Eric didn't even try to remove it.

"I feel like you're failing to appreciate the significance of what I'm telling you," he said.

"No offense, but... what's to appreciate? Some players hardly played and hardly did anything and you found them in that book. Bon appétit," I said, mashing a dunker into the red sauce.

"Yeah, but," he stammered, then paused to get his thoughts in order. "Imagine the stories, Mike."

I would have said, *That's just it. There are no stories. They didn't play long enough to make any stories.* But my mouth was crammed full of a dunker.

"Did they choose to quit?" Eric said. "Did they give

up? Why were they called up to the big leagues in the first place if they were only going to get one at-bat? Was it worth it?" His voice got louder as he talked. "They achieved their childhood dream but then had it taken away after a single at-bat. Did the brief excitement outweigh the bitter disappointment? Have the rest of their lives been affected by their one failed shot at the big leagues? Do they see their achievement as—"

"Eric," I interrupted. "Inhale some oxygen." He hadn't taken a breath in over a minute. "I get it, okay?"

The truth is, I didn't get it at all. Which was a first. Until right then, pretty much every stat Eric had ever shared with me had been really interesting. Our friendship was largely built on his crazy sports knowledge. *Did you know Ted Williams was the last player to hit .400?* Eric might ask me. Why no, I'd tell him. I don't believe I did know that. Go on. *Or that he was given the option of sitting out the last two games of the season so his average didn't dip below .400, but he kept playing?* Nope. I didn't know that either. Anything else? *Or that he went six for eight in those last two games and increased his average to .406?* I didn't. But I'm glad I do now.

Those sorts of stats were different, though. They showed how great the player was. They were examples of incredible feats of skill and talent.

A bunch of Zeros, though? I'd much rather watch better players than worse ones, so why would I care about the worse ones' statistics?

"Really?" Eric said. "You see where I'm coming from?"

"Sure," I lied. "Absolutely."

I picked up a crutch and tried to brush the lettuce off his cheek.

He didn't get what I was doing and swatted the crutch away.

"Be serious for a second," he said, lettuce still attached to his skin. "The potential for some great stuff is there, right?"

"Sure." I nodded. "How many of these guys have you found?"

"I think I'm at six." He tapped his notebook. "Up till now, I've been going about this randomly. Just flipping through the book, hoping to get lucky. It'll be way more efficient if I go page by page."

Page by page? "Sort of sounds like the opposite of efficient," I said.

"Not in the long run," Eric said. "You wanna help me out by writing the names down when I find them?"

"Sure," I said again. "If I can find the time. I did miss two days and have a lot of catching up to do but—"

"Great. You're a lifesaver, Mikey. I already found one I missed. Matty Alou."

Eric started rifling through the book again. "M-a-t-t—"

"You mean right here? Right now?"

Eric raised his eyebrows in confusion. "Any reason why not?"

Because we're in the school cafeteria? I thought. *Because other people have the power of sight and judgment? Because looking through a huge book, one page at a time, sounds like a terrible way to spend the only break we get from our classes?* But I realized this explanation wouldn't make sense to Eric—*who cares what those Butt-something-or-others think?* —and would only risk riling him up again.

"No reason," I said, sliding the pencil out of the metal spirals and flipping the notebook to a blank page. "What was the name again?"

He told me the name plus the position—this guy was a pitcher—along with all his stats. Or his lack of stats, since it was one zero after another.

BY THE TIME THE BUS dropped me off after school, it was at least 3:30. That meant Kirsten had been shooting for about an hour.

My driveway was long, with really big trees hanging over it, and it took me a while to see the hoop.

And to see that Kirsten wasn't there.

Dammit. Had I missed her?

I took a few more crutching steps toward the hoop and felt like crying out loud. Like cussing and bawling and having an Eric-like fit.

Just then I heard bouncing.

I turned.

There was Kirsten, dribbling toward me.

No, not just dribbling. To quote Jake Nichols, the girl was *chugging*.

Right at me, then past me. Going under the basket for a reverse layup.

She rebounded the basketball with her back to me. That was when I realized she was dressed differently.

Instead of a jersey, she wore a shirt with spaghetti straps over the shoulders. Instead of baggy shorts and basketball shoes, she wore jeans and—well, still sneakers.

I crutched toward her and the basket.

"What took you so long?" I said.

I meant it as a joke, but she didn't laugh or even respond right away. When she did, she said, "Sorry."

"Don't sweat it. I was just kidding."

She spun, pivoting on her inside foot, and banked a layup off the board. By the time she caught the ball under the board, I noticed Kirsten's eyes were red and puffy.

Was Kirsten Howard a crier too?

"Everything okay?" I asked her.

"No."

I wasn't expecting her to be so blunt. Just as I started to ask her what was wrong, she said, "I don't want to talk about it."

We both stood there, me clutching my crutches extra hard, Kirsten doing the same with the basketball.

"It's my mom," she finally said.

All I could think to say was "Oh." Which was really lame and stupid, but she said she didn't want to talk about it, and then she started talking about it, so frankly I didn't know what the hell to do.

Then I thought: *How could I not know what to do?* I had a best friend who acted just like this. Except this was different. This was about something real. It was about her mom. Eric got upset about *stuff*—stolen books or bad grades or teasing. But this was about a *person*.

"My parents found out about me skipping class to come here. A neighbor saw me dribbling down the highway and ratted me out. I got outside of the school today and there my mother was—parked right in front like she was on a stakeout or something. She got out of her car and started lecturing me and made me turn around and go inside and change back into my school clothes and go back to class." Kirsten took a breath. "She followed me *into the locker room* and *watched me change*, then walked me to my classroom and stayed there until I went inside."

She stopped talking and squeezed the ball some more.

I had so many questions, I didn't know where to start. Skipping? I thought Dad gave Kirsten a pass to leave school? And hadn't she been getting out of study hall? Could it even be considered skipping *class* when the class was study hall? Besides, shouldn't she or dad have notified her parents before getting her out of school?

I wanted to ask these questions, but if there was one thing I *had* learned from dealing with Eric's crying, it was that logical analysis didn't help anything, at least not right away. Eric had to get the tears out of his system before he could even think about having a regular conversation.

Kirsten kneaded her forehead with the palm of her hand.

"Headache?" I asked.

Eric got them all the time after his teary tantrums. It was the dehydration that did it.

Kirsten nodded, scrunched her face. "The worst."

"A glass of water will do the trick, guaranteed."

She looked up and said, "Thanks, Mike."

I crutched a few steps toward the house. When I got to the path leading to the front door, I looked over my shoulder and watched her put the ball between her knees, slide a hairband off her wrist and put her hair into a ponytail. I watched her shoulder blades tense with the motion of her arms. I was pretty sure I'd never seen them before—her shoulder blades, I mean—and something about them excited me. (So I like shoulder blades. So sue me.)

Her shoulder blades were red—it was getting colder every day—and I half-hollered, "Want a hoodie, too?"

She looked my way and said, "No. As long as I keep moving I'll be fine."

As if to demonstrate, she threw the ball out in front of herself with plenty of backspin, caught it off the bounce, and shot a fadeaway jumper with a little extra arc.

Swish.

The ball bounced back to her.

"Just one more question," I said. "Why did you come here? After all that stuff that happened today—couldn't this get you in worse trouble?"

Kirsten smiled big enough so I could see her too-little tooth next to her front ones.

"Because," she said, "basketball always makes me feel better."

Even when it's basketball that got you into this situation in the first place? I thought. *Isn't that illogical?*

I didn't tell her that, though.

I nodded my head in agreement.

Because I knew exactly what she meant.

WINTER SEASON

"CAN YOU SEE IT?" Dad asked.

"Of course I can see it," I said. "It's right in front of me."

"Yeah, but can you *really* see it? Because your mother"—he jerked his head in the direction of the van, where Mom was sitting— "she says she doesn't see it."

"Dad, do you want to tell me what it is I'm supposed to be seeing? It's cold out here."

Which was an understatement. It was freezing. Literally. The car radio on the way here said negative four degrees. The day before we'd gotten our first snow of the season, but now it was too cold for flakes. A crust of snow covered the baseball diamond to my left and the football field in front of me. It looked crunchy.

It was Sunday morning, the day before the basketball season started for real, and the last thing I wanted to be doing was standing in the parking lot by the football field playing guessing games. Where I wanted to be was in my warm house, moping around because I couldn't participate in basketball tryouts. That's exactly what I had been doing all week and weekend until Dad said we were going on a family trip.

To the high school football parking lot.

"You don't see it, do you?" he said again. "Try squinting."

I sighed steam but narrowed my eyes into slits just to humor him.

Here's what I saw: My dad, at the top of a ladder, looking down at a red, metal, crooked pole sticking out of the asphalt. The pole stood in the entrance to the stadium, between two fences—one that started at the edge of the bleachers, and another that started at the end of the equipment building.

"I see a red, metal pole sticking out of the ground," I said.

I left out the crooked part because there was no reason to rub it in. My dad put the pole there, after all.

He did it last week, three weeks after the JV football season ended, two weeks after the varsity team got blown out in their first and only game of the sectional playoffs.

Dad was apparently the only one who didn't expect this blowout. He spent the next few days moping. This wasn't unusual. Dad's moping, I mean. Especially after yet another disappointing football season. He said he spent too much time preparing to win to be prepared to lose.

"That's it?" he said. "That's all you see?"

When I shrugged my shoulders, he said, "It's not just a pole, Mike."

"What is it then?"

"It's a turnstile." Dad said the word carefully, as though he didn't want to mispronounce it, as though the word was brand new to him and he hadn't been saying it non-stop for two weeks.

As though it wasn't the word that had brought his moping to an end.

"I thought *that* was the turnstile," I said.

It was my turn to jerk my head. On the other side of the ladder, another red metal object leaned against the fence. It was about the same height as the pole. The main difference between the two was that the thing leaning against the fence had spokes sticking out of it. It looked sort of like a metal tree.

"It's *all* the turnstile," my dad said.

"Oh. Okay," I said. "In that case, I see a turnstile. Am I dismissed?"

Dad shook his head. "That's all you see? A turnstile?"

"*Dad.* Do I really have to be here for this?"

He shook his head again. "My own son can't even see it."

I started moving for the red thing with spokes. "You're going to need this, right?"

I got rid of the crutches a week ago, which at first was really exciting. The doctor had said the night I got injured that I could ditch the crutches as soon as I could get around without them, but Mom made me call him and make sure. It took half a day for him to call back, and honestly, I didn't mind having to wait. I was positive I'd gotten the instructions right the first time we met— "You can set the crutches aside when you feel comfortable putting some weight on that knee" were his exact words—and I spent half of the day thinking that maybe I was special somehow, that my body had super healing powers. When the phone call finally came, the doctor confirmed his instructions: "Yes, by all means," he said, "take off the training wheels for a while and see how it goes." Then I asked him what this meant—was my knee healing faster than expected? —and he shattered any and all superpower thoughts. "If you were a long distance runner, maybe," he said, "but otherwise, it sounds like you're right on track. I don't want you making any quick stops and starts anytime soon."

Which was the reason for *my* moping. I'd already imagined making a dramatic entrance onto the basketball court: tossing the crutches aside and sprinting up to my coach and teammates before coming to a last-second, screeching, hockey-like stop that peeled the wax right off the wood floor.

Instead, I spent the first few days of tryouts hobbling around, shooting close-range shots on one end of the court while everyone else scrimmaged on the other. Tomorrow would be more of the same.

And today here I was, standing in the cold, looking at two poles that according to Dad weren't poles.

I bent over and pulled on one of the metal tree-shaped thing's branches. The metal tree-shaped thing was hollow and surprisingly light. I stood it up to its full height, maybe ten and a half feet.

"Here," I said. "Now can we go?"

But Dad wasn't paying attention. He was looking across the parking lot, squinting like he asked me to do, as though it allowed him to see something more clearly.

The car engine sputtered, whined in the cold, revved again. Puffs of smoke came out of the exhaust pipe. Mom sat shotgun. She gazed forward, toward the baseball field. It must have been nice and warm in there, because she wasn't wearing her stocking cap.

I don't think Dad was looking at either Mom or the van, though—or for that matter, at anything else in the parking lot.

"Dad?"

Still no response.

"Dad. Earth to father."

He glanced down at me and grabbed the turnstile with a gloved hand. "Imagine it, Mike," he said—he was doing the squinting thing again— "hundreds, thousands of people coming to the entrance to watch a game. At first they'll be in a line, single file, but once enough people show up it will be too crowded for lines. All those people on this side of the entrance, coming through the turnstile one at a time."

"So you're trying to make it harder for people to enter the stadium?"

"In a way, yes."

Now it was my turn to squint again. "I see many angry people, going home to get their pitchforks. Or to just get warm."

"No, they won't leave," Dad said. "Trust me on that. They might grumble—they definitely might do that— but they won't leave. They'll come back the next week and grumble some more."

"So you're *trying* to piss people off?"

Dad didn't answer. If it hadn't been clear yet, it was

now undeniable: Dad was winding himself up for game-speech mode, which anyone he's ever coached will tell you is his specialty. I looked longingly at the warm car.

"No, Mike," Dad finally said, "I don't want to piss people off, even if that's the result sometimes. I want to make Rapid River football games an event. Something people make plans to attend. Something they show up early for. I want people in this town—not just parents of players, but regular townspeople—to have the Rapid River football schedule up on their fridges. I want the old guys who eat breakfast at *Arnie's* every Saturday to discuss last night's game over their eggs. I even want them to gripe about the imbeciles who are coaching the team."

Dad shook his head and breathed out of his nose. He glanced toward the gray sky, as if he could see the old guys griping up there right now.

"I want what any coach should want for their team: for Rapid River football to be a way of life in this town, an assumed part of all of our daily existence." Dad did another head shake, took another nose-breath. "That's what I want."

It was only then that I realized I was squinting for real, trying to visualize what he was talking about. I opened my eyes fully and pointed to the crooked, red, metal pole sticking out of the asphalt. "And this thing is going to do all that?" I said.

Dad balanced the red thing with spokes on his hip, with one glove around it for support. He put the other glove on the pole. "It'll be a start, anyway. We'll probably have to actually win a few games, too." He slapped the pole like it was a buddy's shoulder. "But I'm telling you, Mike. People like events. They like making a big deal about things if you only give them a chance. And all events include a long line to get in."

I helped Dad lift the thing with spokes high enough to line the bottom up with the top of the pole. When Dad let go, the hollow tree thing slid down the pole like a sheath over a sword.

Dad grabbed a spoke and gave it a shove. The turnstile spun around a few times and stopped. "What do you think?" he said. "Can you see it?"

"Yeah," I told him. "I think I can."

And I meant it, too.

After Dad climbed down from the ladder, we walked back to the car, each carrying an end of the ladder. "How come Mom can't see it?" I asked. "Did you tell her what you just told me?"

"I don't think she wants to see it. She says it's not my job to worry about these things. It's the head coach's. I told her I agree."

This was another sore subject between the two of them. A couple years back, Dad had the opportunity to take the head coaching job—his name was in *The Dais*, our town's local paper, as the top candidate. He'd already turned the girls' basketball program into a winner, and had a Phy Ed teaching job at the school, so it made sense. I think it was pretty much a done deal. But he ended up changing his mind and staying on as an assistant. Mom and Dad did a lot of arguing for those few weeks, and even though they made sure to do it on whatever floor of the house I wasn't occupying, I heard enough to know Dad wanted to take the job but Mom convinced him not to.

This was the first time Dad had mentioned the job out loud since then.

"Plus," Dad said, "I think she's afraid you'll want to play football again."

I looked at my mother, sitting shotgun in the van and staring straight ahead out the front windshield. She was either zoned out or pretending not to notice us out of protest. Either way, she didn't unlock the trunk. Dad had to take off his glove and fish in his pocket for the keys. *She's right*, I thought. *I do want to play football again.*

I could already see myself running onto the field with my teammates as a packed house screamed and cheered and treated our game like the biggest event of the week, just like Dad told me they would.

When I got home and up to my room, my phone told me I had two new messages.

Both from Eric. Both sent over an hour ago.

last day of church b4 the winter mikey???

I replied with two messages of my own.

sorry, dad gave me a sermon of his own haha

p.s. think im playin football again next fall

Eric responded within seconds: cool. im trying out for the baseball team this

spring!!
I typed, really?!
But I thought, uh-oh.

"I think you may be blowing this out of proportion, Mike," Dad said.

"I'm not," I told him.

We were in the van again, on our way to the high school. I yawned. Monday mornings were tough enough even when your best friend *hadn't* recently told you he was trying out for the baseball team. He might as well have said he was having suicidal thoughts.

"I don't know what the big deal is," Dad said. "So Terry's going to try out for the team. Good for him."

Terry was Dad's nickname for Eric. It had to do with Eric's last name, Pendleton, which was the same last name as Terry Pendleton's, a former MVP third baseman for the Atlanta Braves. Eric loved the nickname, of course.

"Dad," I said, "he hasn't played organized ball since fifth grade. He's going to get killed."

"Killed, Mike? I think you're forgetting that baseball's a sport."

"So was being a gladiator in ancient Rome," I reminded him. "And they died awful, gory deaths."

"Any chance you're underestimating your friend?"

Dad steered us onto the exit ramp, getting off highway 12 and getting ready to take a right. Ice glimmered on the ramp. Dad pumped his brakes just in case.

"*Dad*—you were there the last time he played. You of all people should know what I'm talking about."

He was the coach, as a matter of fact. In the first game of the season, he decided to let Eric play catcher. It was the first year of kid pitch, and that meant stealing bases was also allowed for the first time. Eric couldn't catch most of the pitcher's pitches, or even keep the ball in front of him. Pitch after pitch bounced to the backstop. Baserunners galloped from one base to the next. The other team scored 15 runs even though they'd hardly swung the bat. (We didn't technically keep score in fifth grade, but all of us kids kept track.) The other team showed no mercy. Our team got angry. Not at the other team—at Eric. My dad, who didn't know what else to do, finally decided to have me play catcher instead. I'd been sitting on the bench that inning, and when I got up to take Eric's place, Eric lost it.

I think it was getting taken out, not how badly he was playing, that devastated Eric most. He looked up to my dad a lot—and despite all the not-so-subtle comments made by other parents to do exactly what my dad ended up doing, Eric was still surprised when it happened. He'd gotten it in his head as the inning went on and on that he and Dad were in this thing together. That they were going to see it through to the end, no matter what else happened or what the others said.

So when Dad told him to take off the equipment, Eric bawled. Dad actually had to take the gear off for him. First one shin guard, then another, then the chest protector, then… When the mask came off, everyone could see the scrunched-up face that was making the huge howling sounds. As for me, I just stood there, three or four feet away, wondering whether I should put the stuff on or wait until Eric had left the field. No one felt worse than my dad. "I'm sorry, Terry," he kept saying over and over again, under his breath. "This isn't your fault, okay? You didn't do anything wrong. It's my fault. It's my fault that this happened." After that game, Eric's parents took him off the team—and he hadn't tried to play organized ball since.

Until now.

Dad must have been remembering all this, too, because as he took a left past Big Scoop, he said, "That was a long time ago, Mike. I'm sure things have changed a lot since then."

He didn't sound sure, though. He sounded more like he was asking a question than making a statement.

"Not as much as you'd think," I said.

We passed the hospital, just a couple blocks from the high school.

"Anyway," Dad said, "tryouts aren't until the spring. You have a lot of time to talk it over with him."

Which was Dad's way of saying that I had a lot of time to talk him out of it.

At lunch, Eric told me it was a done deal. He was definitely trying out.

"How'd you decide to do this?" I asked, my mouth full of fries. The fries were an attempt to keep my face and voice sounding as neutral as possible. If I could have enunciated more clearly, he probably would have been able to detect the uncertainty in my voice.

"The Bible," he said. He had his hand on the *Encyclopedia* as though he was taking an oath in court. "Its prophets paved the way."

"Prophets?"

"Yeah—all these former players, the ones who only played one game?"

The Zeros.

"Yeah?" I grabbed another handful of fries.

"Well, I've been trying to learn more about them. I didn't know where to start, so I looked them up online— and the only one I could find was this guy, maybe because his name is so unique." He opened the *Encyclopedia* to a bookmarked page. "Ed 'Crank' Crampton, from Oregon. Remember him?"

"Yeah," I remembered writing his name down, anyway.

"He ended up being an American History professor at a small college near his hometown."

"Wow. Interesting," I said, even though it wasn't.

"Here." Eric took his phone out of his pocket, unlocked it and slid it across the table. "Check this out."

"What is it?" I asked.

"Read it."

It was an email.

> *Dear Eric Pendleton,*
>
> *Thanks for the e-mail. No one's called me Crank since well before you were*

"You emailed him?"

"Keep reading."

> *The answer to your first question (why did I only play one game, one at-bat, and so forth), I'm sorry to say, isn't as interesting as you likely hoped it to be. A player got hurt, I was sent up, the player got healthy. There wasn't too much more to it than that. I was a veteran minor leaguer by then, and it didn't surprise me by then to be sent down just as quickly as I was sent up.*
>
> *To answer your other question, however: "Was it worth it?" You bet it was. I had been playing in the minors for seven years by then—riding the bus, staying at cheap motels—and I was ready to move on with my life. But for some reason, I couldn't. Getting called up to the big leagues, flying in a plane, staying at a nice hotel,*

allowed me to move on with my life.

Plus, for the one and only time in my life, I got to use new balls for batting practice.

I hope this email satisfies your curiosity. Thanks again for writing me.

Crank

"Wow," I said again—and this time I meant it. "That's really cool, Eric."

"Not just cool, Mikey. Prophetic."

"What are you talking about?"

"I'm telling you," Eric said, "ever since I discovered these players it's felt like... like I was meant to find them, you know?"

I didn't know. "Eric, the whole church thing, it's a joke."

"Obviously, Mike. I'm not crazy. It *was* a joke. But it *isn't* one anymore. These players—they *mean* something."

"What are you talking about?"

"Until I got this email I wasn't sure, but it seems pretty clear now."

I waited for him to finish his thought.

"That I should go out for the baseball team, Mike. Ever since I quit I've felt like a failure."

"Isn't that a little dramatic?"

"Look, Mike, this is my chance. I don't have to hit

any home runs—I don't even have to get a single at-bat like these guys did. I just have to make the team to… to… to redeem myself, you know?"

He said this as though he was being totally reasonable. Rather than hyperventilating like he usually did when excited, his voice was calm. So were his movements. He reached for his phone and put it back in his pocket.

The thing is, though, he wasn't being reasonable—even if he thought he was. The chances of him making the team were the same as him hitting a home run.

Zero.

It wasn't going to happen. And if he thought it was, he *was* crazy.

I wanted to grab the *Encyclopedia* out of his hands and toss it in the trash like Adam Pilsner.

But I knew Eric would just dive into the bin and fish the book out again.

"HEY, MIKE."

"Oh. Hey, Kirsten," I told her.

I was in my room, holding my follow-through after taking a shot. Kirsten stood just inside the door frame. Moments before, I'd been counting down slowly from ten before attempting the game-winning shot. I'd used my best announcer voice as I described myself as "the sharpshooter from Rapid River."

I really hoped she didn't hear me say that.

"Did it go in?" she asked. "Did the sharpshooter from Rapid River live up to the hype?"

I dropped my arm. "No," I admitted. "But I got fouled. The refs are still looking at the replay to determine whether I got the shot off in time."

Kirsten made her hands into fists and pretended to bite them. "The suspense is killing me," she said.

I laughed. "I didn't realize you were here today."

She nodded. "Coach Duncan texted me and said he had a few things to go over with me before Monday's game."

"Wait," I said, genuinely surprised. "Coach Duncan texts? As in my dad?"

The guy may have been a visionary as a coach, but when it came to technology, he had always been a dinosaur. Years ago, when Mom was trying to convince him we needed a family plan, she said that it was crazy in this day and age not to have a cell phone. "This day and age?" Dad replied. "What's so special about this day and age, Mary? They seemed to get along okay without cell phones in every other day and age in the history of humankind." Texting has always been particularly annoying to him. "What's so hard about calling someone?" he liked to say. "Are we so busy in *this day and age* that we can't have an actual conversation?" We ended up getting the family plan as a gift to "all of us" from "Santa."

"I showed him how to do it last week," Kirsten said. "I think it takes him about a day to finish typing. I can't believe he still has a flip phone."

It's true. Year after year our cell phone company tells him he's due for an upgrade; year after year Dad says it's not worth the hassle.

"So maybe you were supposed to be here yesterday, not today," I said. Then I panicked: *what if she didn't realize I was joking?* "Don't get me wrong," I said, "you're welcome here whenever you want, no matter what my mom says."

Which I realized was a stupid thing to say as soon as it came out of my mouth.

"She doesn't like me, does she?" Kirsten said.

"No," I stammered. "I mean, yes. Yes, she likes you. She just doesn't—she doesn't get the whole sports thing."

Kirsten entered the room enough to close the door behind her. "I know, right?" she said. "What is it with parents and not getting sports?"

I knew she wasn't talking about parents generally. She was talking about hers. But I still didn't know what to say. I didn't mind her complaining about them, but joining in felt risky.

"You know that you were making the lights blink?" Kirsten said. "We were downstairs, me and Coach, and the ceiling was, like, *thudding* every time you jumped, and then the light started flickering." She laughed—in disbelief, I guess—and said, "It was kind of freaky."

I shrugged. "What can I say? It was a pretty epic game."

"Must mean your leg's getting better, huh?"

"Yeah—I have another doctor's appointment coming up. Hopefully I'll get cleared to practice."

"Definitely," she said. She took her hands out of the front pocket of her hoodie. "So . . ." she said, "can I play?"

Before we started, I told her she needed to know some ground rules. How to dribble, for instance. (The ball didn't bounce too well, so you were allowed to throw it down off the carpet and then catch it—so long as you kept throwing it down and catching it in one continuous motion. You could never just hold the ball while moving.) How to shoot a three-pointer. (At least one body part had to be touching the desk—your back, the back of your legs, the heel of your foot, etc.) How to block without goaltending. (Since it was relatively easy to jump up and touch the ceiling, the defender was not allowed to stand back and block three-pointers.) How to foul (make any contact with the arm or wrist), and how not to foul (any other contact was completely acceptable).

These rules, I told her, were invented and approved by the commissioners of the International Bedroom Basketball Association.

"Let me guess," she said. "You and Eric?"

"And Dad," I said. "He's like the James Naismith of bedroom basketball. Dad played a version of this game with me when I was a kid, but Eric and I are in charge of any and all subsequent rule changes."

"Pretty big responsibility," Kirsten kidded.

"It's a tough job," I said, "but somebody's got to do it."

"How do I know you haven't rigged the rules in your favor?"

"Any objections," I said, "should be addressed in a letter to the commissioners of the International Bedroom Basketball Association."

"Sounds reasonable," she said.

Then she took off her hoodie to reveal a tight, black, stretchy shirt underneath. "Okay if I take a practice shot first, commissioner? It might take me a while to get the hang of this."

It didn't. Within a few minutes, she was pump faking and shooting quick-release three- pointers and was already getting plenty of backspin on her shots. She did the dribble-catch thing like she'd been doing it her whole life.

She was physical, too. She dug her heels in on defense and pushed back against me when I tried to move to the basket. On offense, she put her shoulder and butt into me and backed me toward the hoop.

Finally, as she leaned into me, making shimmy-fakes while pivoting one way and then the other, it happened.

I didn't know if it was her butt grinding against me, or placing part of my forearm against her chest whenever I had the ball—either way, when I looked down, there it was.

It was, simply put, the most terrifying thing that has ever happened to me in my life.

I turned away from Kirsten and mumbled something about the bathroom. Swearing under my breath at my tired knee to hurry up, I escaped my bedroom and crossed the hall and dragged my leg into the bathroom, slamming the door closed behind me.

Go down! I muttered. *Go down, dammit!*

But minutes passed, and it wouldn't budge.

I flushed the toilet, turned the water on and off, and took the only option I had left: I trapped it with my waistband against the part of my stomach just below my belly button.

Luckily, I was wearing a baggy shirt.

When I got back to my room, Kirsten had her long-sleeved shirt back on. "I better get going," she said. "I guess I lost track of time."

She made her way to the door, and I wondered if she

was shuffling along the edge of the dresser that way to keep as much distance from me as possible. Had she felt it pressing against her? Did she know?

"You're too tall," she said. "Next time we play, you have to use your head to block shots. No more hands allowed."

I said, "Okay" and watched her leave.

As I gathered up and re-stacked some *Sports Illustrateds* that had fallen off the dresser during the game, I let out a deep sigh and waited for the blood to start flowing to all the other parts of my body.

JAKE NICHOLS WAITED FOR ME in the hallway again at the end of fourth period.

"Looks like that's getting better," he said, tilting his hair toward my knee.

"Slowly but surely."

"Hardly limping at all," he said. We passed the school library, a big circle-shaped room in the middle of the school. "I bet you won't miss a beat on Friday."

We entered the hallway that led to the cafeteria. "Friday?"

"Yeah, the Winter Dance," Jake said. "You're going, right?"

"Oh. I'm not sure. Like you said, the leg . . ."

Truthfully, my leg had nothing to do with my not wanting to go. It just provided a convenient excuse. Up until then it never crossed my mind that I'd go to this or any other dance. Just thinking about dancing in front of others was excruciating. I'd spent the last three years of junior high avoiding dances, and I didn't see any reason to start going now.

"Nikki will be totally bummed if you don't go," Jake said.

"Nikki?" I said. As in Nikki Paulsen, a girl I'd hardly ever spoken to in my life?

"Yeah, man," Jake said. "She's got a serious thing for you." We entered the cafeteria and I spotted Nikki sitting at her usual table. Another girl, Abbie Clausen, was drawing something on her palm with a pen. They were both laughing. Jake must have noticed me looking at her, because he said, "What do you say, man? Put the poor girl out of her misery and come ask her to the dance."

"I'm not sure . . ." I stammered. "I mean . . . it's just . . . I don't know . . ."

"Look. Is it Eric? Is that the problem?"

Truthfully, I hadn't even thought about Eric. But I was glad to be given the excuse.

"I'd invite him too," Jake said. "But I really don't think it's his sort of thing. Besides, I don't know who he would go with, you know?"

Jake was being a dick—I knew that. But then again, I didn't entirely blame him, and he wasn't entirely wrong. Eric really wouldn't have a good time at a dance. And it was hard to imagine any girls were sitting at Jake's table pining for some Pendleton.

"I better at least talk to him," I told Jake—because I couldn't think of any other way to get out of the situation.

Eric was already there when I got to my table. As usual, he had placed his backpack on the table and the *Encyclopedia* on his lap. I sat across from him and stared at the backpack.

"Hey, Eric," I said.

He was so absorbed in his reading that he didn't hear me.

"Hey, Eric," I said again.

He mumbled a hey back, still reading. I thought he might have mumbled something else, too, but I didn't hear him and didn't ask him to repeat himself.

I was too busy thinking about Nikki Paulsen.

Who, according to Jake, had a thing for me.

I didn't exactly know what qualified as a *thing*, or why she would have one for me. But I did know that it was the first time anyone had ever told me a girl had a thing for me, and I'd take what I could get.

Had she been talking about me to other people? What had she been saying?

"Mikey. Mikey. You there?"

I re-focused and saw Eric staring at me. He had taken the backpack off the table without me noticing.

"Oh, hey. Sorry."

"Did you hear what I said?"

"Hear you say what?"

"That I was going to California for winter break."

"Really? Why?"

"To see my relatives, supposedly." He made his fingers into quotation marks so I knew that wasn't the real reason. "I'm *actually* going so I can play baseball outside. My uncle said he'd hit me as many grounders as I wanted. It'll give me a leg up at tryouts this year."

"That's great," I said. Of course, I didn't think it was great at all. In fact, I all of a sudden felt an irrational hatred for his uncle, who as far as I was concerned was only making it less likely that Eric would come to his senses.

I changed the subject. "Hey, maybe we could try sitting over there sometime."

"Where?"

"There." I gestured to my left. "With Jake and John and those guys."

"Butt Clan Central?"

"Not all of them are that bad," I said.

But Eric wasn't listening. He reached under the table. When he sat up again he had his backpack.

"Suit yourself," he said. "Sit wherever you'd like."

He set the backpack between us.

I wasn't sure if he was mad at me for wanting to hang out with his enemies, or for hardly reacting when he announced he was going to California. Either way, right then I didn't truly care.

After all, Nikki Paulsen, a real live human girl, had a thing for me. And if one real live human girl could have a thing for me, it suddenly seemed more possible that another could, too.

WHEN DAD PULLED INTO the driveway that evening, Kirsten sat shotgun. I hoped she would be. All day I had been thinking about the dance—about how for the first time ever I actually wanted to go.

Not with Nikki—with Kirsten.

I didn't even know if Kirsten liked dances. Would her dress be the same fabric as her jerseys? Would it have her name and number on the back?

For that matter, I didn't know if she liked *me*. I mean, I knew she didn't *mind* me. But saying yes to a game of one-on-one was different than saying yes to a dance. Right?

There was only one way to find out.

"You coming to my game on Friday, Mike?"

Kirsten was out of the car and holding up her hands for the ball. I passed it to her.

"You have a game on Friday?"

Kirsten nodded. "It's away."

"If you twist my arm," Dad called as he entered the

house, "I'll even let you do the shot chart."

Wow, thanks, Dad, I thought as the door closed behind him.

Kirsten launched a shot all the way from the edge of the garage. It clanged off the rim and she chased after it. "Seriously, though. You should come."

"I'll do my best. I was invited to this dance later that night but—"

Kirsten cut me off: "Some girl roped you into that, huh?"

No. I mean sort of. I mean, I don't want to go with some girl; I want to go with you.

That's what I would have said if Kirsten didn't add: "For once I have an airtight excuse not to go. I'd rather run killers in practice than go to a dance."

She launched another shot. This one bounced off the rim and then rolled in. By the time I rebounded the ball, Kirsten was heading back through the garage. "I have to go study film," she said. "Seeya, Mike."

I started to say, "Seeya" but she was already gone.

The more I thought about my conversation with Kirsten, the angrier I got. I wasn't mad that she said no to the dance—because she *hadn't* said no. She hadn't even given me a chance to invite her. She'd immediately assumed that some other girl had, in her words, "roped me in." (Why couldn't I have done the asking? Why couldn't I have been the roper inner?) And—here was the worst part—she hadn't seemed at all jealous. She was just glad that she didn't have to go with me.

Okay, I was adding the *with me* part. She didn't say she didn't want to go with me, just that she didn't want to go at all. With anyone. But I was upset enough that it was hard to see the difference.

No, I decided. I wasn't going to do the shot chart at the game.

Because I wasn't going to the game.

I was still upset the next day, when I found Jake in the hallway and said, "I'm in for the dance on Friday."

"Great, man," he said. "You're making a certain someone a very happy lady."

"About that. Do you have her schedule? Should I ask during lunch?"

"Don't worry, man," Jake said. He clapped my shoulder. "I'll take care of it."

IT DIDN'T HIT ME until twenty minutes before Jake picked me up that I didn't know what I was going to wear to the dance.

And even then it only hit me because Mom asked, "What are you going to wear to the dance?"

I was up in my room shooting hoops. "Clothes, Mom. I'm going to wear clothes."

I took another shot. *I'll wear my suit and tie,* I thought—*the same one I wore to band concerts last year before I quit playing the trombone.*

It was my only formal clothing, so it wasn't a very tough decision.

"I'm only asking because if I were you I wouldn't wear your suit and tie," Mom said.

"And why is that?" I asked, trying to keep my voice casual. Seriously—how did she do that? Was she telepathic or something? I took another shot.

"Well, for one thing, you've grown a lot since you last wore them."

Good point.

"And for another, I'm just not sure it's that kind of dance. You said it's in the gym, right?"

"Yeah," I said. I was starting to get concerned. "What would you suggest?"

"I got these for you on the way home from work."

It was only then that I looked at Mom and realized she was holding a plastic bag.

"What's in there?"

"Just a collared shirt and some pants," she said, walking across the room and setting the bag on the bed. "The girl at the store said they would make you look cool."

Mom always sounded ridiculous when she used words like cool.

"I didn't know your size—all you ever do is wear your hooded sweatshirts and warm-up pants—so I got several pairs. Maybe you can try them on and we'll return whichever ones don't fit?"

As it turned out, Mom was a lifesaver. When Jake picked me up—he honked his horn instead of knocking on our door—I saw that he was wearing basically the same thing as me: a lined collared shirt (his was red, mine was blue) and khakis.

"Hey, man," he said after pressing a button to lower the window on the shotgun side of the car. Jake's car was nothing to write home about—a Buick something or other that must have been at least 10, 15 years old. Still, it was hard not to be jealous. I didn't turn 16 until the summer, so any hope of having my own wheels was months away. "Hop in the back, would you?" Jake said. "We still have to pick up Kel."

Kel was Kelly—Jake's date for the dance.

I opened the back door and found my date sitting there, her hair piled up on her head.

"Hey, Mike," she said. "I'll scoot over."

She had already unbuckled and scooted before I thought to offer to go around to the other side. Her dress was dark blue and sparkly and in two pieces. As she slid across the backseat, her top lifted and revealed a little of her midriff.

I said thanks as I got in, which was the first time I'd talked to her since—well, I don't remember when the last time I talked to her was.

I never even officially asked her to be my date to the dance.

Somehow that was already taken care of by the time I got to school on Tuesday. John Atkinson came up to me that morning and said, "I hear you're taking Nik to the dance on Friday. Treat her right, man. She's like a sister to me." He said it sternly, then offered his fist for me to pound and said, "I'm just playing, Mike. I'll see you at the dance."

Then Jake asked me if I wanted a ride and I said sure, and just like that, my dance-related responsibilities were over.

I pulled my seat belt over my shoulder and tried to think of something else to say.

As the four of us—Jake, Kelly, Nikki and I—walked from the parking lot to the entrance next to the gym, I wished I'd brought my sports coat after all. Or, even better, my winter coat.

Not for me. For Nikki.

It was freezing, and therefore I was freezing, and therefore Nikki must have been in danger of hypothermia. Her dress was strapless, and her shoulders were going white to red before my eyes.

"Are you okay?" I asked. "I mean, you must be pretty cold, huh?"

Captain Obvious to the rescue.

"You're sweet," she said. "But I'm fine."

Or at least I think that's what she said. Her chin shook too much for her to talk clearly.

The parking lot had patches of ice and snow all over the place. Jake, who was in the lead, did his best to navigate around them as the girls took wobbly steps in their high heels. As we stepped up to the sidewalk, Nikki lost her balance and grabbed my shoulder. The hand felt like ice through my shirt, but it felt kind of good, too, especially after she'd recovered her balance and hooked her arm around mine.

Finally, we made it to the side entrance and walked arm in arm into the building.

Which ended up being the only time I touched Nikki

all night.

Honestly, why did she even want to go to the dance with me? Maybe she didn't—not really. Maybe she just wanted to go with my arm. Maybe that's why they call it "going to the dance" instead of "spending the night together at the dance." Maybe she just needed a guy's shoulder, elbow, wrist, and hand for a few minutes as she entered the gymnasium.

Our arms were still hooked as we walked through the darkened gym together. The basketball hoop had been raised to the ceiling on the far end, and there was a DJ station, and everyone clumped together, shifting to the music. Once we got to the fringes of the clump, Nikki broke away from me and started hugging all the girls and exchanging compliments about each other's dresses. Evidently, my arm was no longer needed.

For a while, Nikki and some of the other girls danced in the same general area as me and some of the other guys. But it was clear right away that most of us couldn't keep up.

This wasn't true with all the guys. Some made-up dance moves as they went—they mimicked sprinklers, lawnmowers, and various other appliances. Others— most of them in the middle of the clump—touched and pressed and grinded against their dates. One guy, Richard Breimhorst, was on the fringes of the clump like me, but unlike me, he continuously twirled two or three girls at once. There was a line of girls forming to get twirled by Richard. (Note to self: when and if I ever go to another dance, I need to learn how to twirl girls.)

Most of the guys' idea of dancing, though, was to

hunch their shoulders and every now and then pick up a foot and set it back down.

Don't get me wrong. I'm not judging.

I was one of them.

No, that's an insult to them. I wasn't even graceful enough to be included in *their* dance circle.

Because that's what the "clump" of people turned out to be—bunches of little circles, seven or eight to a circle, divided largely by degrees of confidence and skill.

And everyone seemed to be a part of some circle, except me.

There I was, standing on the outside, alone, hunching and picking up my feet and trying to make my body move naturally to the blaring rhythm of the music.

I swear the floor had better rhythm than I did.

Which was more than a little frustrating. This was the most time I had spent on the basketball court in a year. All my life the court had been the most comfortable place in the world to me, but now it had turned against me.

A slow song started, and for a brief second, there seemed to be hope. All you needed to slow dance was the ability to shuffle your feet.

That, and a date.

After a moment I spotted mine.

Dancing with John Atkinson.

His arms were around her waist. I'm an only child, but the things he was doing with his hands didn't look very brotherly to me.

At some point, I announced to no one in particular that my knee needed a rest and I walked across the court and out the gym doors.

There was a drinking fountain there. I dipped my head, slurped.

"Hey, Mike."

I knew the voice, but I didn't believe it. Had Kirsten Howard decided to come to the dance after all?

I wiped my mouth with the back of my hand. "Hey."

If she had, she was a little underdressed. She was in her Rapid River basketball uniform and had a ball trapped against her hip. Her forehead was chalky from dried sweat.

"What are you doing here?"

"Just got back from the game."

"How'd it go?"

"Okay," she said.

"What was the score?"

"64-37."

"Sounds like it went better than okay."

"We played a lousy first half—then turned it on in the second. We've got to play the whole game if we want to go anywhere this year."

By anywhere, I knew she meant the state tournament. I looked over her shoulder.

"Where's everyone else?"

"Changing into their dresses. Hey, any idea when this dance gets over?"

Now it was her turn to look over my shoulder.

"Think it'll be a while," I said.

"Shoot. I was hoping to work a little on my tear dropper." She set the ball in her hand and looked upward at an invisible rim. A tear drop shot is where you're in the lane and shoot the ball nice and high before the defender is expecting it. "I got blocked today by their big girl," Kirsten said, her eyes returning to me. "My family leaves for Florida tomorrow. If I don't fix the problem now I'll be thinking about it my whole winter break...."

She trailed off as if what she said explained everything: why she was here, after a win, hoping to practice her game instead of hanging out with friends, or pack, or sleep, or do anything that anybody else does on a Friday night.

I knew about the trip to Florida. She mentioned it yesterday before Dad brought her home—and she didn't sound happy about it. Mom and I were sitting at the dinner table, and she told Kirsten to have a great time. "Not likely," Kirsten said. She wished us happy holidays and then Dad drove her home.

"It's dark in there," I said, pointing my thumb at the gym. "But one of the hoops is still down. I'll stand there and act tall if you want."

"Are we even allowed in there?" she asked. She brushed by me, opening the door to the dance a little at a time like she was prying it open to trespass on someone else's property. She looked back at me and smiled. "Only one way to find out."

I followed her inside.

The two of us spent the rest of the dance at the empty end of the gym. I stood by the basket with my arms straight up as she pushed into me, stepped back, and shot one high arcing shot after another over my outstretched hands.

Maybe dances weren't so bad after all.

AT DINNER THE NEXT NIGHT Mom was in the best mood I'd seen her in for a long time. Which wasn't surprising. She always got this way around winter break. She made ham tonight. Originally, she bought it for Christmas Day, she explained, but decided, "Oh, what the heck—we can always get another one if we want to."

Dad and I both complimented her on the food, and for once she accepted the compliments, reaching her arms in opposite directions and touching our arms. "Thanks, men," she said.

She still had her hands on our forearms when the doorbell rang.

"I got it," I said, wiping my mouth with my napkin.

"Thanks, man," Mom said. She didn't say *man* like Jake Nichols did; she said it as an extension of her previous comment. It was her idea of a joke.

Yeah, my mom has a weird sense of humor.

And I'm not going to lie: it was nice to see her making jokes again. It had been a long time since she was in this sort of mood. Especially with dad around. It's not like I'd never seen them get mad at each other before—but the last few weeks had been pretty rough.

I got up from my seat and walked down the hall and opened the door.

"Kirsten?"

For the second time in the last two months, tough-as-nails Kirsten Howard was crying.

"Are you okay? I mean, aren't you supposed to be in Florida?"

"I couldn't... couldn't miss a week and a half," Kirsten said. Despite her tears, her voice was strong. "Not when the season is just getting going. Not if I'm serious about going to the state tournament. I told my mom I couldn't go, and that I wouldn't change my mind, but she wouldn't listen, wouldn't believe me . . ."

She trailed off, wiping her puffy eyes as though she was angry at them.

"Can I come in?" she said. It wasn't so much a question as a statement: *I'm coming in.*

I stepped aside and watched her shed her boots on the carpet. I was about to offer to take her coat but she was already marching down the hallway, coat and stocking cap and mittens still on. All I could do was follow her to the dinner table.

Mom looked up. "Kirsten?"

"Hi, Mrs. Duncan. Coach."

Mom was too stunned to say anything else. Dad nodded. Why wasn't he more surprised? Had he known that she wasn't going to Florida?

Kirsten repeated what she told me: she'd talked with

her parents and decided she couldn't go a week and a half without touching a basketball— "We have way too much to work on." She looked at Dad, who gave her a sympathetic half-smile and another head nod. "The last thing I should be doing is taking a break. We're just getting to the important games. I'm not going to risk coming back rusty."

The last few remarks weren't directed at anyone, I don't think—at least not anyone at the table. She was looking at the ham in the middle of the table, although I don't think she actually saw it. It was like Dad squinting in the parking lot while patting the turnstile: Her voice sounded distant, as if she was talking to herself or repeating an earlier conversation.

She kept looking in the direction of the ham until Mom said, "Do your parents know you're here?"

Kirsten's eyes shifted to Mom. "I'm staying at Abby Robertson's. I just wanted to let you know I'll be around during the break and—if it's all right with you, Coach— I'd really like to keep doing what we've been doing."

Dad nodded his head one more time.

"Okay," she said. "I better get going."

She marched down the hallway again, eyes straight forward, as if she had accomplished her mission for the night.

I followed her down the hallway and watched her jam her feet into her boots. "Do you need a ride?" I asked.

"No," she said, voice still matter-of-fact, pulling at her boot laces with her mittened hands. "It's just a few blocks."

"How about some help tying those?"

Finally, she broke.

She even laughed a little.

"Yeah," she said, dropping the laces and holding up her mittened hands. "Some help tying these would be good."

I knew this wouldn't go over well with Mom. I knew that we would spend the rest of the meal eating in silence. I knew that Mom's good mood had already vanished. And I felt bad about all of that. But in that moment, while tying Kirsten's boots, I mainly felt excited. And relieved. Up until a few minutes ago, I thought I was going to spend my winter break alone. Eric on one coast, Kirsten the other.

In my mind, she was already long gone.

But then, just like that, she wasn't gone at all. She stood right here in my entryway. And she'd be here for the rest of the break.

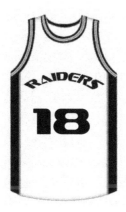

KIRSTEN SAID THAT FIRST NIGHT that she was staying at Abby Robertson's house—but it would be more accurate to say she was sleeping there.

Because most of her waking moments were spent at our place.

After a few days, a schedule developed:

Kirsten arrived just after breakfast. (The first day she had to knock; after that, we left the door unlocked for her.) She and Dad spent an hour or so in the basement as soon as she arrived, then another hour before dinner.

The rest of the time she hung out with me. Mom had to work until Christmas Eve, and Dad was home but stayed out of our way. When Kirsten and I were upstairs, he would be in the living room; when we were in the living room, he would be in the basement.

The two of us played bedroom basketball until the window fogged up.

We played one-on-one on the driveway as long as our cold hands could stand it.

We watched old basketball movies that no one else our age had probably even heard of ("The Pete Maravich one, *The Pistol*, was my favorite growing up," Kirsten told me) and re-read Mike Lupica sports books ("Oh my gosh. I *loved* these as a kid," she said).

We looked up *The Guinness Book of World Records*. ("Longest fingernails," she quizzed me. "Easy," I said. "Lee Redmond. Altogether, over twenty-eight feet of nails." Kirsten looked at the picture and shook her head. "That chick is gross," she said.)

We did all the things, in other words, that I usually did with Eric over winter break. I'd like to be able to say I missed Eric during those couple weeks—but I didn't. Not really. Having him out of sight made it easier to forget about his plans to try out for the baseball team. The first few days he was gone, he texted me with updates: *uncle says i have good fielding range* and *guess who just made an over-the-shoulder catch?* I didn't reply to these texts, though, because I didn't know what to say. If I encouraged him, he'd just get his hopes up even more. If I told him the truth—*everyone who tries out will be able to make an over-the-shoulder catch, Eric*—I'd just come across as a jerk.

Luckily, paying attention to Kirsten made it easy to ignore Eric.

On the night before Christmas Eve, we played mini-baseball in my living room. I went over the rules: first base was an arm of the couch; third base was an arm of the recliner. I used masking tape to make second base and home plate, which was in the corner of the room, just enough in front of the Christmas tree to allow for full extension when swinging. Anything on or over the kitchen table was a home run, I explained. Anything under the table was a ground-rule double.

"Let me guess, these are the official rules, Commissioner Duncan?"

"Oh," I told her, "and another thing: You have to play on your knees."

(This last rule was invented by my dad years ago during the World Series. At the time Eric and I thought it was just to add another quirky element to the game. But Dad has since confessed that he came up with the rule so he could see the TV. "Win-win," he said. "You guys could keep playing, and I could keep watching the World Series.")

"Is that a great idea?" she said, pointing to my knee. She was genuinely concerned.

"That's why I'm wearing this," I told her. I slapped my heavy-duty brace.

She swung the little wooden bat I got as a kid for being one of the first thousand fans at a Minnesota Twins game. "Just one question," she said. "Don't we need a ball?"

"Oh... I suppose that would help, huh?"

This was usually Eric's department. He always brought a little round foam ball from his house. I think it was originally ammo for a Nerf gun.

I looked around the room as if a little round foam ball might show up on a tabletop if I was patient enough.

"I have an idea," Kirsten said. She was already on her knees, and she reached behind her and took off one of her anklet socks. "Give me that tape."

I handed it to her and she wrapped the masking tape around and around her bunched up sock. Once all the cotton was covered, she tossed the tape-sock ball to me. "How's that?"

I tossed it up and down a few times. "It's practically the same size as a real baseball," I said.

"So I guess we're playing mini softball instead," she said and walked on her knees to the plate. "I'll hit first."

Four innings later, we heard the garage door open. Mom was home.

That meant it was almost time for dinner—and for Kirsten to go back to Abby's.

"Last pitch," Kirsten said. "Winner takes all."

"How does that work?"

The score was tied—5-5—with nobody on.

"Simple," she said. "If I hit a home run, I win. If I don't, you win."

I started swinging my arms back and forth like the old-time pitchers did as they wound up to throw. "I like my odds," I said.

"Just pitch the ball, Meat," she said.

After several more arm swings, I did. Right over the plate. Kirsten swung and hit a line drive that ricocheted off my brace and wedged under the far side of the couch. By the time I moved for the ball, Kirsten had touched the arm of the couch and was on her way to second. I scramble-crawled along the couch, tugged the sock-ball out and turned for home.

Kirsten touched the arm of the recliner and kept going.

More scramble crawling.

The two of us lurched for home plate at the same time. Me to block it, her to touch it.

We collided and the next thing I knew we were lying in a heap—her on top, me on the bottom.

"Did I win?" she said.

"Did you even touch the plate?" I asked.

"I'm not sure. Did you touch me with the ball?"

"Not sure."

"Hmmmm," she said. I had the ball in my right hand, which lay at my side. She pinned my wrist down with her knee, lowered herself a little more so her upper body was parallel to mine but not quite touching it, and slapped home plate. "I guess I did win after all," she said.

Her face was just above mine, and I thought how easy it would be to kiss her—but then, over her shoulder and over the couch, I saw Mom emerge from the hallway with a bag of groceries. If she saw us, she didn't let on, but I must have made a startled face or something because Kirsten was off me and standing up in less than a second.

"Hey, Mrs. Duncan," she said. "I was just beating your son at baseball. Hopefully, he's not too depressed to eat tonight."

Mom looked at her, and then looked over the couch at me on the ground. "Something tells me he'll recover," she said.

Then she asked her usual question about whether Kirsten was staying for dinner. Kirsten gave her usual thanks but no thanks and headed for the hallway. The only difference was that this time, she was missing a sock. I was still lying on the living room carpet, but I could hear every other step make a suctioning-slapping sound on the linoleum.

I got up and made it to the entryway in time to see her jamming her barefoot into a boot.

"Want your sock back?" I said.

"What sock?" she said. "All I see in your hand is a mini softball."

She had everything on including her mittens, which she pounded into place with the insides of her thumbs.

"Sorry you didn't get a chance to work with Dad tonight," I said.

"I'm not," she said. She clicked the door handle and pulled. "I mean, if we lose the state tournament I'm going to blame you, but..." She shrugged her shoulders. "I can live with that if you can."

She smiled—little tooth and all—and stepped out the door.

FOR THE FIRST TIME ever, Christmas morning sucked.

At first, it seemed pretty normal. We all took turns opening presents—from each other and then from "Santa," also known as my mom. My haul was pretty awesome, actually: tickets to a Timberwolves game (Dad), another nice collared shirt (Mom), and a letter jacket (Santa). I'd wanted a letter jacket since I was a kid, and even if it didn't have any letters on it yet, I couldn't help imagining it decked out with a giant R and a handful of medals. That's what I was doing when Dad opened his gift from "Santa"/Mom: tickets to the musical *Rent*. "Hmmmm," Dad said, "I think Santa might have given herself a present here, huh?"

By the time I looked at Mom, her eyes had already misted over. "I'm sorry to be so selfish," she said, her voice deep with sarcasm. "It gets worse, Jeff. I thought you might enjoy taking me to a musical."

Dad protested that that wasn't fair—he'd clearly been joking—but she stormed out of the room anyway.

I had gotten used to hearing them argue, especially these last few months, but this was worse. I'd never seen Mom so fragile.

It was stupid. I mean, as far as I could tell, Dad was right: he'd obviously been joking. She should've laughed the joke off and said something equally sarcastic. That was what she usually would have done. And the fact that she didn't do that scared me.

At some point, Dad got up too. I thought he was going to follow her upstairs, but he didn't. He went downstairs instead.

An hour later, when Dad emerged from the basement, Mom was still in their room. Dad went straight for the fridge and got the fixings for a leftover-ham sandwich. He dug through the fridge, muttering something about mayo.

"Dad?" I said, entering the kitchen. I waited, and when he didn't turn around, I said it a little louder. "Dad."

He turned, mayo bottle in hand. "Hey, Mike. What's up?"

"What's going on?"

"What do you mean?"

"Between you and Mom. Are you two okay?"

I was embarrassed to ask the question. It somehow made me feel younger and more helpless.

He unscrewed the top of the bottle. "We had a fight, Mike. Sometimes parents do that." He turned and went for the silverware drawer.

"I know, but . . . is that all?"

"What do you mean?" he asked again.

"I mean, that fight . . . it was different. Should I be worried about anything?"

"Not that I know of." He held up a butter knife as though he'd made a discovery.

When he took his eyes off the knife, he saw that I was still standing there.

"Look, Mike," he said. "What do you want me to say? I'm not worried, so you shouldn't be either."

"You've spent Christmas in different parts of the house."

"Yeah, but we're still in the same house, Mike. I'm not going anywhere and, as far as I know, neither is she. We love each other—we love you—too much to go anywhere, okay? Okay?" he repeated.

I nodded my head and said sure.

Dad took the knife to the counter and spread the mayo over a slice of bread. Once the sandwich had been made and the knife had been put in the dishwasher, he walked by me, patted my shoulder, and took his sandwich to the basement.

A few hours later I was in my room—lying on my bed, shooting my mini-basketball toward the ceiling over and over, trying to zone out and think of only the ball and my hands.

"The basket's that way."

It was Kirsten. She was already halfway into the room, a gym bag strapped across her shoulder.

"Good tip," I said to her. I pretended to look at a

watch I wasn't wearing. "Short meeting with Dad."

"Yeah," she said. "Hey—is everything okay? Coach Duncan seemed a little . . . distracted."

"Things are fine," I said. "Mom and Dad just got in a little fight." I changed the subject. "What's with the gym bag?"

Kirsten smiled. "This isn't a gym bag. It's wrapping paper." She pulled the strap off her shoulder, dropped the bag to the carpet and unzipped it. "Merry Christmas, Mike," she said, tossing something at me without looking up.

The white object spun at me like a Frisbee. I grabbed it out of the air.

"A volleyball knee pad?"

"Correction," Kirsten said. "It *used* to be a volleyball knee pad. *My* volleyball knee pad." I could see that; it had sweat stains on it. "Now it's a mini softball knee pad. So you're not so lopsided when you're wearing your brace."

"Wow. Thanks," I said with mock excitement. "It's what I always wanted."

She shrugged. "What can I say. When you're good you're good."

"Wait until you see the gift I got you," I said.

"Oh, yeah? And what's that?"

"No guesses?"

"Quit stalling," she said.

She was right—that's exactly what I was doing. Not that I was trying to hide it. I made a show of scanning the room with my finger tapping my lips, trying to spot something, *anything*, to give her.

"I'm not stalling. I'm building the suspense."

"Ahhh. I was wondering if that's what you were doing."

I thought of what she got for me: a knee pad for my uncovered knee.

Bingo.

I pulled off my right sock, bunched it up, and threw it to her. "Merry Christmas."

Her eyes and mouth opened wide. "A used sock. How did you know?"

"Something told me you needed a replacement."

"It's perfect," she said. "Thanks, Mike."

Except the thanks wasn't dripping with sarcasm—it was sincere. Not sincere about the used sock being just what she wanted, but I got the feeling she wasn't just talking about the sock. She was thanking me for... well, me.

And just like that, I felt really nervous.

We stayed there like that—her standing and staring at me, me sitting on the bed and trying not to break eye contact—until she said, "I better get going" and kneeled down to zip up the bag.

I got to my feet and said, "I'll walk you out."

"Great," she said.

I stood over the bag as she pulled the zipper. Before the bag closed all the way I saw a used copy of Bill Russell's autobiography, *Going Up for Glory*. I had seen that book before.

"Did Dad lend you that?" I asked, pointing at the

book.

"If by lend you mean *gave*," Kirsten said, "then yes. You Duncan men, you sure know how to pick out Christmas presents for a lady."

THE FOUR REASONS I hadn't tried to kiss Kirsten yet:

> 1. I was chickenshit.
> 2. I was chickenshit. (Can't emphasize this enough.)
> 3. Now that Kirsten's family was back, I didn't see as much of her.
> 4. I had a plan.

This plan had everything to do with the date:
December 31st.
New Year's Eve.
Just a few hours until the clock struck midnight. And the whole world locked lips.

I couldn't take all the credit for the plan. Jake Nichols was the one who got me thinking about New Year's. He called a few days ago and invited me to a party at his place.

"Nikki's gonna be there, man," he said. "If you play your cards right, you could be her New Year's kiss."

Or, more likely, I could watch her play tonsil hockey with John Atkinson.

"Thanks," I told Jake. "But I'm busy."

It was a simple plan, really. Earlier on the 31st, I had unzipped Kirsten's gym bag. I found *Going Up for Glory*, the book dad had given her, and opened it. Clearly, Kirsten had been reading it: she'd earmarked her page, which was toward the end of the book.

I fished in my pocket for the note I'd written: *Meet me in the driveway, 11:59 sharp.* I put the note in the book, on the same page Kirsten had earmarked.

Mission accomplished.

Or at least that's what I thought until later that night.

I stood outside my house, alone, looking down my driveway—waiting. I removed a mitten and took my cell phone out of my pocket. 11:52 pm.

It was only at this point that I began to see all the potential problems with my plan. There was so much I hadn't considered: What if she didn't feel like reading today? Or didn't feel like sneaking out of the house for a late-night stroll along the highway? What if she opened the book and found the note and had no interest in following its instructions? Or what if she did follow the instructions, and I kissed her, and I sucked at it. I was a sophomore in freaking high school who had never kissed a single girl—a fact that had never seemed as embarrassing as it did right then. Up until fairly recently, I'd been a shrimp who would have had to jump to reach most girls' lips—of course kissing was going to be awkward, not to mention unlikely. But now I didn't have any excuses. What if I was as clumsy with my lips as I was at dancing? What if I was such a bad kisser that afterward we both wished it hadn't even happened but knew that it had and could never be comfortable around each other again?

You're being too dramatic, I tried to tell myself. I removed my mitten, checked the time. 11:56.

Before I had come outside, I turned the floodlight on over our garage. Most of the basketball court was lit, but after that, the driveway got dark quickly. Patches of ice shined at the edge of the light, and the dry spots of asphalt looked like pitch-black puddles.

It was as if the court was an iceberg, floating in an Arctic sea.

The thing was, I wasn't being *that* dramatic. It was terrifying how one wrong move could send two people drifting apart. Yeah, my parents had been fighting for a long time, but at least they had still been talking. At least they still acknowledged each other's presence. Now? My dad made one lousy joke at Christmas and ever since it was like my parents were invisible to one another.

I had been watching TV with them before I came outside. The camera kept flashing around to all these people huddled together and smiling in the cold. When

I scanned my living room, there was none of this excitement. Mom sat to my left on the couch; Dad sat in the recliner. The two of them watched all the noise and cheers in absolute silence. When the commentator announced that it was ten minutes to the new year, I got up and waited for one of them to call my name and ask where I was going.

But neither of them did, because they were both sleeping.

"I'm not going anywhere and neither is your mom," Dad had said—and the words had become a mantra in my head. So long as no one left, they could work it out. *We* could work it out.

When I walked out the front door I slammed it shut and hoped it would startle them awake. I spent most of my childhood watching the ball drop on TV with Mom and Dad and telling them to get a room when they kissed—but this year I almost wished I was going to be there to see it happen.

I stared at the island of light some more as I took off my mitten to grab my cell phone—11:59 on the nose. As I put the phone back in my pocket, I heard dribbling.

It was dark enough that I couldn't actually see Kirsten, but I thought she might be able to see me. I was back by the garage door, but the light was probably on me—and I wondered if it was like peering into the dark with your bedroom light on. You can't see out, but if anyone's out there they can see in.

I was just beginning to make her out when the ball stopped bouncing.

"Hey," she said. "Did I make it in time?"

She stepped into the court.

I stepped forward, too.

"So…" Kirsten said, "did you want to get beaten in one last game before the end of the year?" She dribbled a few more times. "Is that it?"

"Maybe later," I said. As if that made any sense.

"Not sure there is a later," she said. "I bet we have like twenty seconds left. You're not stalling, are you?"

I kept stepping toward her.

I couldn't think of a single thing to say.

Kirsten pulled up her sleeve and looked at a watch that wasn't there. "Make that ten seconds," she said.

And with that my internal clock started the countdown.

Eight… seven… six… I was only a few feet from her now. *Four… three… two…*

"At first," Kirsten said, and for the first time she sounded a little nervous, "I thought the note was from Coach Duncan."

Eeeeeeeeehhhhhhhhhhhh! the buzzer in my head blared.

I was just about to lean in—I swear I was—but her comment stopped me. Probably because the last thing I was expecting to hear about as I kissed a girl for the first time was my dad.

So instead of leaning in, I leaned back. "Oh, yeah?"

"Yeah—I mean, the note was in the book he gave me, and"—she still sounded nervous—"and it wasn't signed or anything, so… I was thinking, *what could he want at 11:59?*"

Pause. Awkward silence.

"That would be pretty strange," I finally said. And because I didn't know what else to do, I grabbed the ball from her and said, "Shoot to decide who starts?"

When she didn't answer, I turned and saw her hit herself on the forehead with her eyes closed. Keeping her hand on her forehead but opening her eyes, she said, "That was a pretty dumb thing to say, huh? It's just that… I've never kissed a boy before—which is probably also a pretty dumb thing to say right now, especially if you *weren't* planning on—" She didn't finish her sentence, instead opting to just say, "Sorry."

I could have told her it was okay, or that I had never kissed anyone, either, or—

But it seemed easier to step up to her again, and put my mittened hands on her cheeks, and lean in all the way this time.

The two of us stood there, on our iceberg of light, celebrating the new year as it's supposed to be celebrated.

Later that night, I looked at my phone and realized Eric texted me.

can't think of a better way to spend new years than breaking in the glove i got for xmas!!!

I didn't text back, but if I had, I would have written: *I can.*

IT TURNED OUT THAT KISSING was an acquired taste.

In all honesty, that first kiss on the driveway felt weird. Her lips felt different than I'd imagined. Mushier or something.

What if there's something wrong with me? I thought. *What if I'm the first person ever to not like kissing?*

But then she kissed me again.

Kissing may be an acquired taste, but I'm happy to report that it's acquired really fast.

Now that we had started kissing, it didn't seem like we were ever going to stop.

We kissed every day after her meeting with Dad. If both our teams were practicing at the high school, we kissed before and after entering the gym. If one of us had a home game and the other didn't, we'd wait for each other outside the locker room, lips ready to go.

For three years I had complained to Eric about all the PDA (Public Displays of Affection) going on at school. I had muttered, "Get a room" under my breath repeatedly. But I guess I was just jealous. Because suddenly I was PDAing repeatedly and without remorse.

I was the president of the PDA.

I wasn't just a PDA employee; I was also a client.

I was the star player on the Rapid River PDAers.

You get the idea.

It was the post-game kissing I liked best. Especially when it was Kirsten who had just played the game. I was back on the team now, and that was great—but it had been almost a month since I returned, and I hadn't yet touched the floor in a game. I was pretty sure the place I sat on the bench had begun to form indentations that perfectly matched the contours of my rear-end.

It wasn't as if my teammates were begging Coach to let me play, either. I'd been playing with them since we were in elementary school, and I'd never been much of a difference-maker. Skilled, sure. Good enough to get some court time, absolutely. But not someone who made much of an impact one way or the other. They didn't say it, but some of them might have even been a little angry that Coach had reserved a spot for me over their friends.

Of course, the real problem was our record. Unlike the football team, we weren't terrible. In fact, being terrible might have been easier to take. Instead, we were good enough to compete against most teams we played, but not quite good enough to pull out many wins.

And it was hard to be revved up about anything— even kissing Kirsten Howard—after watching my team lose yet another heartbreaker.

On the other hand, Kirsten's season was still going

strong.

To say the least.

So far, the Rapid River girls' varsity basketball team hadn't dropped a single game.

In mid-January, they beat Pine Hill, their biggest conference rival. The next week they beat Lakeshore, who was ranked second in the state at the time. Their next game was against Eagle Creek, and practically our whole town showed up to cheer the team to victory.

Part of the team's popularity, I suppose, had to do with the boys' team's mediocrity.

Part of it had to do with the high-octane, fast-breaking, full court-pressing style my dad had the girls playing.

But most of it had to do with Kirsten. By the time they beat Pine Hill, Kirsten had been athlete of the week in our local paper, *The Dais*, four times. She'd been athlete of the week in the city paper twice. A week ago the city paper ran an article on her. Dad was quoted as saying, "No disrespect to anyone else, but she's the best player in the state, and I'm not sure it's all that close."

"Yes, Coach Duncan might be biased," the article concluded. "But having seen her play, this humble reporter finds it hard to argue with him. And only partly due to fear of repercussions. (Note to Kirsten's Krazies: I'm on your side!) Don't take our word for it, though. Go check her out yourself, if you can find a ticket. Don't worry: you have time. Kirsten's only a ninth-grader."

Kirsten's Krazies were our self-titled student cheering section, who showed up to every game and held up signs with Kirsten's name on them. Against

Lakeshore the senior guys spent the entire first half shirtless, their chests painted with the letters of her name. You might think that a group of older high school guys stripping to the waist for my girlfriend would make me insecure, and if I'm being completely honest it did— but it was also pretty cool to know it was *my girlfriend* they were stripping for if that makes any sense. During halftime, our athletic director, Mr. Morris, told them they could either put their shirts back on or leave the game and never come back. (When I told Kirsten about this, she was furious. "Wait," she said, "you're telling me they can show up shirtless in the *freezing* cold during a football game but not at a girls' basketball game?" I assured her I wasn't telling her anything, just reporting what Mr. Morris had said.)

Of course, I was as swept up in the craziness as everyone else. I had been since the first day I saw her play.

During her game against Eagle Creek, I sat across from Kirsten's Krazies and the rest of the student section. The section was even louder that day because the boys' basketball squad—sophomore, JV, and varsity—had the day off and showed up for the game. Every once in a while I looked up and saw Jake's hair bobbing and Nikki laughing toward the back of the section. But mostly I watched the game.

Like everyone else, I didn't want to miss whatever Kirsten was going to do next.

This one went down to the wire. Eagle Creek was winning by a point with six seconds to play. Coming out of a timeout, Rapid River got the ball around half court.

Dad had Kirsten throw the inbounds pass. Some of the people around me were angry: *How could Kirsten be passing the ball in?* they wanted to know. *Shouldn't she be the one trying to get open for the pass?*

I wanted to tell them to relax. The point of the play *was* to get Kirsten the ball. She'd pass it to someone—probably Heather Stern, the other guard, in the backcourt—then run and get the ball back with just enough time (hopefully) to make a move and go to the basket.

The Eagle Creek coach put her center, all 6'2" of her, in front of Kirsten. The center's long body and arms would make it difficult for Kirsten to see who was open. At least that was the idea.

Dad was concerned enough that he considered calling a timeout to call another play. I watched him start to put his hands together in a T before his assistant coach pulled his arms down.

No timeouts left.

The referee handed Kirsten the ball, and the Eagle Creek center waved her arms wildly in the air.

Janet Pederson, our center, flashed to the free-throw line, and I knew Kirsten wanted to get the ball to her. If Eagle Creek's center was guarding Kirsten, someone smaller had to guard Janet.

Except Kirsten couldn't possibly get a pass up and over this girl's outstretched arms. Not one with any zip on it. So she went under them instead. She faked a pass over the top and then, her eyes and chin still high in the air, made a no-look bounce pass between the girl's legs.

Janet caught the ball on the second bounce, and I

thought she was going to make a move to the basket.

I think *she* thought she was about to make a move to the basket, too.

She set her pivot foot and started to raise the ball in the air.

But right then Kirsten streaked by her, took the ball out of her teammate's hands and—using Janet's body as a screen—went in for a game-winning layup.

It happened that fast: Kirsten, seeing she had a bigger, slower player guarding her, had followed her pass to Janet, racing around the Eagle Ridge center to take the "handoff" from Janet.

The crowd erupted. So did Kirsten, and Janet, and the rest of the team. They jumped around and hugged as people rushed the court. I stayed where I was, though. Everyone wanted to get a piece of Kirsten, to clap her on the shoulder and congratulate her—and while they did that, I walked down the bleacher stairs and went the opposite way, away from the court, to the hallway that led to the locker rooms.

Usually, by the time she came out of the locker room (she was always one of the last to leave), Kirsten was happily exhausted. She was excited about the latest victory but also completely wiped out. And the combination of the two gave her a certain calm. We would sit near the locker room door where she couldn't be seen by the parents and fans who were waiting outside to do more shoulder clapping and autograph seeking. (It was mostly younger girls who wanted her to sign their program or jersey, but not entirely. Plenty of older kids and even adults had shoved markers and programs at her as she got in her dad's car and left the high school.) Once she summoned the energy to meet her fans, Kirsten would turn her head and plant her lips loosely on mine, then stand up and walk down the hallway with me toward the people and the parking lot.

But the Eagle Creek game was different.

She didn't sit next to me.

She pounced *on* me.

She skipped out of the locker room, jumped up and pushed her lips against my lips, her teeth against my teeth—and I swear, she *growled* at me. I could feel it leave her throat and vibrate in the back of my mouth.

We both leaned our heads back. I think we were equally surprised.

"Whoa," I said. "Where did that come from?"

"I don't know," she said. "I wasn't trying to do it. It felt good though, right? Weird, but good."

I nodded.

"Weird but really good," I said.

THINGS WITH KIRSTEN WERE going great—unlike everything else in my life…

For one thing, I was still riding the bench during games.

For another, nobody seemed to be talking to one another.

Mom still wasn't talking to Dad.

Dad still wasn't talking to Mom.

("I'm not going anywhere, and neither is your mom," I kept repeating in my head. "I'm not going anywhere and neither is your mom." "I'm not . . .")

Even Eric and I were hardly chatting during lunch. Mainly because the one thing he wanted to talk about— baseball tryouts—was the one thing I didn't want to talk about. The best I could give him was one-word answers. When he told me he'd been working on the slide step while turning the double play at second, I said, "Nice." When he told me his swing extension was getting way quicker through the zone, I said, "Cool." Honestly, I wasn't even sure he noticed our lack of conversation. On the one hand, his obliviousness was a relief. It let me off the hook. But it was also irritating. How could *he* not care that *I* didn't care? If he was my best friend, shouldn't he have been able to know what I was thinking? To know something was off? With his comments? With my life?

Along with the *Encyclopedia*, Eric spent lunch working on his new glove. "Gotta break it in somehow," he said as if it was totally normal to *sit on a baseball glove* in the middle of a high school cafeteria.

Kirsten and I talked all the time, of course. But not about Eric. And definitely not about my mom and dad. Which was a little unfair, I suppose. After all, she told me all about her parents. Especially her mother, who was still pissed about Florida because she couldn't understand how anyone could choose sports over family. I told her that some people just couldn't understand the importance of sports, but even though I was pretty sure she knew I was talking about my mother, I didn't elaborate. I didn't say, "At least your Mom is still on speaking terms with you. My mom pretends my dad's not even there." Dad was Kirsten's coach, after all. I didn't want to put her in an awkward position.

Besides, I've never really been good at sharing my feelings. It's not just me; it's my whole family. Clearly, my parents didn't want to talk to each other or to me about their relationship, but then again, they almost never did. We almost never did. Some people like to talk about personal stuff—to analyze every feeling they have, whenever they have it—but not us. If you don't say anything for long enough, the problem usually goes away on its own, you know?

This was a little different, though.

Part of me *did* want to talk with Kirsten. Just not yet. *Maybe someday,* I thought, *in the future, when Mom had finally forgiven Dad and everything had finally blown over between them, maybe then I'd mention their rough patch to her.* It actually felt good to imagine having this future conversation with her, because it implied that 1) things were definitely going to blow over between my parents, and 2) Kirsten and I were going to have a future together.

Of course, at the time, I had no way of knowing that Kirsten's and my future was going to be so short.

When Kirsten came outside after her meeting with Dad, she was startled to see me. She paused on the front walkway before putting her head down and walking toward me.

"Hey," I said, holding my basketball. I thought she was going to show me her hands so I could pass her the ball. But she didn't. She just kept walking with her head down.

"I have to go home," she said, and hustled right by me, her face turned away.

I walked after her a few steps and put my hand on her shoulder. "Can't Dad drive you today?"

She flinched at my touch. "No. I mean, I can walk myself."

"Everything okay?"

By then she was ten feet away from me. "I have to go, okay?" she said over her shoulder.

I started to follow her, but she sped up.

"Wait up," I said.

She didn't. "I'm sorry, Mike . . . I have to go," she repeated.

Just like that, she broke into a run. A few seconds later, she was long gone.

I went inside, knocked on the door to the basement, shouted down to him.

Finally, he answered. "What is it, Mike?"

"Is everything okay?"

Pause.

"Everything's fine, Mike."

Did his voice sound different? More strained or something? "It's just that Kirsten—"

"Kirsten left a few minutes ago."

"I know. That's why I'm—"

"Look, Mike, I'd rather not shout. I'll be up in a little while, okay?"

But he wasn't up in a little while. I sat on the couch for more than an hour before Mom saw me and asked me what I was doing just sitting there with the TV off. I didn't really know what to tell her—she'd been angry enough about the Kirsten situation without adding more fuel to the fire—so I shrugged my shoulders and headed upstairs.

When I got to my room I tried texting Kirsten.

Should I be worried?

After an hour, I tried again.

We can talk after your game tomorrow if you want? And again.

Or we can just hoop. Meet me in the driveway tomorrow night? Or the next day?

Finally, at some point—I'd fallen asleep with my clothes on—my phone buzzed.

Don't think I'll be going to your house anymore. Sorry.

DAD DROVE ME TO SCHOOL.

I asked him what was wrong with Kirsten and he said she'd be fine.

"Then why did she say she wasn't coming to our house again?"

Dad watched the road intently—too intently? —but couldn't help wincing. "She said that?"

I waited for him to answer my question.

"Look, Mike . . ." he said, but then he just repeated himself: "We had a difficult conversation, okay? My guess is that it has something to do with that."

"A difficult conversation about what?"

"I'd rather not talk about it, Mike. I'm sorry, but I hope you'll respect me on that."

Kirsten had apologized to me, too. As she raced away from me. And then again in a text message. Which is supposed to be a nice thing—saying you're sorry—but what does it mean when you don't even know why the person is apologizing?

"So that's it?" I said. "Kirsten's never coming to our house again—sorry?"

"Give her some time, okay? I think she may have gotten a little carried away."

I didn't bother asking what she may have gotten carried away about.

Luckily, that day at practice I didn't have too much time to dwell on Kirsten or Dad or whatever the hell happened the night before.

I was too tired.

We had lost our last game, against Pine Hill, because of missed free throws. With less than a minute to go, we were up by enough points to force Pine Hill to start fouling us to stop the clock. If we'd made the free throws, we would have won easily—but we missed them, and Pine Hill made a few big buckets down the stretch to come back and win.

As a result, we did only two things at practice:

We shot lots of free throws.

And we ran.

Coach Wight had all of us stand at the baseline. One at a time, a player stepped forward to the line and shot five free throws. However many baskets the shooter missed, that's how many killers we ran.

Let's just say we missed a lot of free throws.

All of us held our hips and hunched over, our breaths wheezy. My body was so tired it didn't know what to do with itself. I sweat and shivered at the same time. I was totally dehydrated—my lips were so dry they stuck to my teeth—but way too tired to drink anything (assuming Coach ever let us take a water break).

Disclaimer: when I say *we* missed free throws, I'm not actually talking about myself. I don't say this to be a bad teammate—there's no I in team, blah blah blah—but just to point out that I hadn't had the chance to miss (or make) any free throws yet. Besides, not to brag, but if there was one thing I could do, it was shoot free throws. In junior high, there was an annual local free-throw shooting competition. I won it three years in a row. Actually, just shooting, in general, was my thing. If basketball were just a game of H.O.R.S.E., I'd be a superstar. The problem has always been getting—in other words, getting off—my shot.

But no one tries to block your shot when you shoot a free throw.

"Duncan, you're up," Coach Wight said.

I wondered if I had blacked out for a second. We'd been going right down the line, and last I'd checked, there were still three guys ahead of me, including Jake Nichols, who stood next to me, bent over at the waist.

"Coach?"

"Step up to the line, son."

So I did. I straightened up and accepted the ball from Coach Wight and pressed the toe of my right foot just behind the free-throw line. I cleared my head, which wasn't difficult. I was too tired to think, anyway. Then I followed the same routine I've been following since I was eight and Dad put up our hoop in the driveway.

I stretched my neck, dribbled three times, spun the

ball against my palm—never taking my eyes off the rim. The ball left my fingertips with my elbow pointing the way.

Swish.

I took my eyes off the rim just long enough to receive another pass from Coach.

I took a breath and started my routine again. Almost all basketball players learn that you should establish a free throw shooting routine, but there's more to it than that. The routine only matters, my dad taught me, if it gets you in a rhythm. Take Tim Duncan, my Dad once told me. Besides being one of the best shooting big men ever, he follows the same free-throw routine over and over, and yet somehow manages to not be a good free thrower. And it's all because he takes this really long, rhythm-breaking pause before he shoots. ("Or at least that's my theory," Dad said, "and I'm sticking to it. For some reason he never called and asked me to be his free throw doctor.")

After my three dribbles and ball-spin, I let another shot go.

This one touched a little rim, but also buried itself in the net.

Another key to shooting free throws is wrist and elbow strength because unlike your legs, your wrist and elbow don't get tired, or heavy, or weak.

Neck stretch, three dribbles, spin the ball, shoot.

In again.

Some part of me was conscious, of course, of my teammates. I saw them straightening up more and more with every make, their chests heaving less and less. But that was only when I lowered my eyes to get the ball back. After that, it was all about the rim again.

I made the last two and didn't need a rebounder: the shots had enough backspin to bounce back to me on their own.

Someone actually clapped his hands, as if he was a fan or something.

The next player in line was Adam Pilsner. When he stepped toward me to take the ball and the next five shots, there was audible groaning. This was definitely a first: Adam may have been a butthead bully to Eric, but he was pretty popular. Maybe because everyone was afraid of him. He was a big bruiser of a guy who routinely knocked other players to the floor, including his own teammates.

He was also a terrible free throw shooter.

As he approached me, the rest of the team shuffled to the baseline, getting ready to run.

I handed the ball to Adam just as Coach Wight said, "I have an idea. Why doesn't Mike take the rest of the shots today? We'll save the running until the end."

The rest of the team didn't say anything, probably for the same reason I didn't: they weren't sure whether this was a trick question. If we said yes, would he say basketball is a team game and we failed his little test? What was the catch here?

Which was what I almost asked Coach when he said, "Duncan? That work for you?"

"Whatever you say, Coach."

"You can go back with the others, Pilsner," Coach said. "Duncan, the amount of running your team does for the remainder of practice is entirely dependent on the number of shots you miss." He stood with his back to the rest of the guys as he said this. "Got it?" He finished with a wink.

"Got it, Coach," I said. Because I did: he wasn't putting me on the spot to be cruel. He was giving me a chance to win over my teammates and truly earn my spot on the team.

Maybe if I made enough free throws, I thought, I might see some playing time. Maybe I would even start some games.

But I was getting ahead of myself.

First things first.

I stretched my neck, took my dribbles, spun the ball and sunk another shot.

That evening, as I walked up the driveway, I typed a text message to Eric: *you'll never guess who got booed today at practice...* (Okay, Adam didn't get booed, but close enough.) I was just about to type the answer (Buttbreath? Buttcrust? I could never remember which was which) and hit send when I looked up and saw Dad's car in the garage. This was a surprise. He had a game that night. That was why Kirsten had stopped by the night before: to study film of their next opponent.

The game wasn't until later that night, but he never came home between school and a game.

I was confused. But I was also excited.

I couldn't wait to tell him about practice.

After all the crappy stuff that's been happening in this house, here was some news we could celebrate together.

I'd made 14 of my last 15 free throws. Even the one I missed was in and out. By the end of practice, my teammates cheered every single make. A couple of them actually stood under the basket and caught the ball before it had a chance to bounce on the ground. They'd look up through the rim and watch the ball drop into it, then throw me a chest pass and tell me to keep it up, man, whatever you do, don't stop now. When I was done, my shoulder and backside were slapped repeatedly, and my fists were banged by other fists.

I sidestepped Dad's van and opened the door to the house. "Dad?"

"In here."

I found him in the kitchen: sitting at the table, holding a newspaper.

"Aren't you supposed to be at a game right now?"

Dad lowered the paper but I didn't give him a chance to answer. "We had practice today, which—well, duh, you knew we had practice—but at practice, we were shooting free-throws—"

"Mike."

"—and every time we missed we had to run. But then Coach called on me, even though it wasn't my turn, and—"

"Mike," Dad said again, this time with a little more force. I stopped talking. "I need you to read something, okay?"

He folded the paper, twice, and extended it to me,

the pointer finger of his other hand showing me where to start.

It was our local paper, *The Dais*. He pointed to the Letters to the Editor section.

"What's going on?"

"Just read this, okay? We'll talk about it when you're done."

I followed his finger to the first letter, which was only a paragraph long:

> Our daughter, Kirsten Howard, plays on the varsity girls' basketball squad.

I looked up.

Dad looked away.

I kept reading.

> Over the past school year, her coach, Jeff Duncan, has developed an inappropriately intimate relationship with her. For the last few months, he has met with her one-on-one every night after practice—a decision which we questioned at the time but unfortunately allowed to continue. Recent events have confirmed our worst suspicions: that this relationship has gone well beyond what is appropriate for a coach and his high school player. We've chosen to go public with this letter in the hope that actions will be taken more swiftly.

Sincerely, Linda and Steve Howard

I had finished the letter but wasn't sure what to do next, so I read it again. My eyes snagged on the phrase "inappropriately intimate" and wouldn't budge.

Finally, I said, "What does this mean?"

"It means there was a misunderstanding."

"A misunderstanding of what?"

"Of our relationship. Of Kirsten's and my...." He didn't finish the sentence. "Look at me, Michael." His hand was on my shoulder, and he didn't say anything until I lifted my head from the paper. "None of it is true, okay? Whatever it seems to be implying, it didn't happen. That's why I wanted you to read it now, with me sitting here. I wanted you to hear me tell you right away that this is completely untrue."

By now he had both his hands on my shoulders and was leaning in, his eyes watery, his voice shaking.

"Are you hearing me?" he asked. "This isn't true, Mike. Okay? Whatever it's suggesting, it isn't true."

I believed him. Of course I believed him.

He was my father. Why wouldn't I believe him?

SPRING SEASON

DAD RETURNED HOME LATE that night. I was up in my room, lying on top of the covers with my clothes on. The door to the garage opened and closed. "What else is there to say, Gary?" my dad said.

"If that's all there is to it, Jeff—"

It was Mr. Morris' voice. Rapid River's Athletic Director. I recognized his voice because he had called the house a few hours earlier looking for Dad.

"Of course that's all there is to it, Gary."

"Well, then you'll have to say that publicly."

"*Of course* I'm going to say it publicly."

"Have you thought about legal representation?"

"Jesus, Gary. A lawyer?"

A lawyer?!

"I can't believe you coached that game, Jeff."

"What are you talking about?" my dad said. "Why wouldn't I coach the game? I didn't do anything wrong, so—"

"I'm sure that's true. But until this gets cleared up, I have to suspend you, Jeff."

"What? For a misunderstanding? That's insane."

"I'm sorry—but it's my job. I'm worried you still don't understand the severity of the accusation made against you."

"Of course I do, Gary."

"Well, then you know you had no business going to that game."

"No, I don't know that. How many times do I have to say it? This was a misunderstanding."

"I hope so. Look, I believe you, Jeff."

"Why *wouldn't* you believe me?"

"I said I do. But I have to tell you, if you go anywhere near the school or the team before this issue is settled, I'll be forced to fire you. I'm surprised, Jeff. Someone as smart as you are about image and marketing should know that your best move is to step down *voluntarily* until this matter is resolved."

All of this was happening so fast, I didn't know what to think or do. How could a misunderstanding lead to all of this? Dad was right: Mr. Morris's words were insane. How could suspending him be for his own good? It was odd, though: he didn't *sound* insane. His tone of voice was even and unemotional. It sounded as if he was being totally reasonable.

"Jesus, Gary," Dad said again. "I'll set the story straight tomorrow. Okay?"

Another silence.

"I just don't understand how you could have let her go down to your basement, Jeff. How the hell could you have done that?"

"It wasn't like that, Gary."

"Like what?"

"The way you make it sound. Like the basement is my *lair* or something. What's the matter with you?"

"I'm stating the facts. You let her go down into the basement with you. Can't you see why that's not a good idea? Can't you see why people don't like the sound of it? Are you truly claiming to be that naïve?"

"Would you be saying this if the player wasn't a girl?"

Dad's voice sounded like a challenge.

"That's not the point—"

"Would you, Gary? Because what you're saying is that a male coach has to treat his female player differently—"

"I'm not getting into this with you. Now's not the time—"

"Now is the *perfect* time, Gary. Isn't what you're saying straight-up sexism? Answer the question: would you be saying this if I'd been watching film with a male basketball player?"

"I don't know. Maybe not. I mean, there was what happened at Penn State, but—"

"Penn State! Now you're accusing me of being Sandusky?"

Sandusky. Jerry Sandusky. The Penn State football coach who did all that. . . stuff. . . to those boys. . .

What the hell was happening right now?

"Calm down, Jeff."

"You're seriously asking me to calm down when you're accusing me of—"

"The only thing I'm accusing you of is being unbelievably naïve."

"So you're saying you believe me."

I could hear Dad taking deep breaths. Then I realized I was doing the same thing.

"Yes. I believe you. I want to believe you, Jeff."

"Which is it? You believe me or you *want* to believe me?"

Yeah. Which was it?

"I'm not the one you have to convince, Jeff. They're going to look into this—"

"They?" my dad interrupted. "Who are they?"

"There's Naïve Jeff again. We don't have time for him. You know who *they* are. Cops. Investigators. The people who look into this kind of thing are going to do precisely that. And they should. Can you not see that? I need you to see it. I need you to publicly *encourage* them to look into this. Do you really want to live in a world where a letter like that isn't investigated?"

"I'm not saying the accusations aren't serious, Gary. I'm saying they're not true."

"Okay, good. So when you give your side of the story," Mr. Morris said, as if there were multiple sides to the story, "I'd advise you to make a sincere apology."

"An apology? An apology for what?" my dad said, his voice suddenly loud again. "A misunderstanding?"

"If that's how you want to think about it, sure.

Apologize for contributing to the misunderstanding."

"Jeff Duncan apologize? Not in our lifetimes." It was Mom's voice. She'd arrived home around dinner time, as usual. I had heard the garage door going up and realized I didn't want to talk with her about the letter. I thought about bringing the paper with me, but then decided that that would be pointless. If she didn't read the news in the paper, one of the reporters who kept calling the house would fill her in. I'd been up in my room ever since, and Mom hadn't come looking for me. "Jeff Duncan is a lot of things, Gary," she said, "but he's not an apologizer."

"Hi, Mary," Mr. Morris said. "I hope we didn't wake—"

"Tell him, Jeff," she interrupted. "Tell Gary that you will never apologize, no matter what happens."

"Not if I didn't do anything wrong, Mary," Dad said. "If that's what you mean. I won't apologize if I haven't done anything wrong."

"Exactly. See, Gary? Apologizing is admitting wrongdoing—and Jeff? Jeff Duncan? He'll never admit to wrongdoing because he's never wrong. Are other people affected? Are they hurt? Is his whole family now going to get raked over the coals for something that was preventable if he'd just put his family first for once in his life?"

Raked over the coals? What was that supposed to mean?

A door slammed.

Then: nothing. Silence.

My thoughts filled the silence.

I thought: What's that word again?

Collateral damage.

I thought: Am I collateral damage? Is Mom? Is Kirsten?

I thought: What does it mean to be collateral damage in this case?

I thought: *Case.* Is that what this is? A case?

I thought about me.

I thought about Mom.

I thought about Kirsten. Did she play in the game today? Or had she been in her room, trying to avoid everything and everyone like I was?

I thought about her running down the driveway, getting away as fast as possible. Away from what?

I thought: *so-called* misunderstanding?

I thought: What. The Hell. Is going on?

BEFORE, NO ONE WAS TALKING to me.

Now, no one was talking *around* me, either.

And I don't just mean Mom or Dad or Eric or Kirsten. I mean *everyone*.

Now that my dad had "taken a leave of absence" -- that was how Mr. Morris said he'd describe it to the media--I had to ride the bus to school. When I got on, the bus was totally silent. Maybe everyone was just groggy—it *was* 7:30 in the morning—but that's not what it felt like. This was a different kind of quiet. A thicker quiet. The kind of quiet that happens when someone's been talking loudly about someone else then shuts up just as that person enters the room.

After fourth period, I saw Jake Nichols. I thought he was waiting for me, but I was wrong. I watched his hair bob down the hall, past the library, toward the cafeteria.

Eric sat at our usual spot in the lunchroom. He had his baseball glove on and threw a ball into it over and over again. A girl sitting at a table five feet from him flinched every time the baseball smacked into the glove. I didn't blame her.

He was concentrating so hard on what he was doing, he didn't notice me. I walked right by him and headed for the hot lunch line.

He kept tossing the ball into his glove as I set my tray down across from him. He must have heard the silverware clatter on the tray because he finally acknowledged my presence.

"Mikey! How are you?" His voice was loud. When I didn't answer, he said, "I saw the article. Do you want to talk about it?"

"Would you keep your voice down?"

Truthfully, it wasn't the volume of his voice that was the problem. It was the concern in it. The seriousness of his voice made it impossible not to think of the situation as serious.

Which is exactly what I'd been trying to do all day.

"It's just a big misunderstanding," I said, my voice even louder than his. I felt the need to make a public announcement: *It was all a misunderstanding people! Please resume your regularly-scheduled lives.* I wanted to reassure everyone: Eric, the others in the cafeteria, even myself.

"Yeah. I mean, that's what I assumed."

"Assumed? What does that mean?"

"Nothing, Mike. All I meant was—"

"You've known my dad your whole life."

"No, of course, that's not what I was saying—"

"Just drop it," I said.

Eric lifted his shoulders and let them slump. "Sure, Mikey. Absolutely. Whatever you want."

It was almost funny. All day I had been unintentionally muting people the second I got near them. Then someone finally talked to me—and it was my so-called best friend—and all I wanted him to do was shut up.

Next thing I knew, he had his backpack on his lap and took out the *Baseball Encyclopedia*. "Maybe the prophets have something wise to tell us," he said, risking a smile.

He took the notebook out of his backpack and slid it halfway across the table.

"They're not prophets," I said. "They're baseball players." They weren't even *that*, really. They were *bad* players. They were nothing but Zeros.

Eric's smile went away. "Sorry," he said. "Just trying to lighten the mood."

I didn't say anything.

His hand remained on the notebook, and he slid both back to himself. We sat there silently for a while, then Eric opened the *Encyclopedia* and buried his head in it. Which also pissed me off, even though I knew it wasn't his fault. The kid couldn't win. I didn't want him to ask me about my dad. I didn't want to help him with his *Encyclopedia*. And I didn't want him to read the damn thing, either.

At some point, Eric looked up from his book and said, "Hey, do you want to go to the batting cages after school with me and my dad?"

"I have practice."

"I mean after that."

"I probably shouldn't," I said. "Mom and Dad probably want me home."

"Yeah," Eric said. "You're probably right."

Even *that* pissed me off. I didn't want him to sound so understanding. It felt condescending or something.

When he went back to his book, I got up and threw away my entire tray of food. Tray included. Which I immediately regretted. Doing something so drastic wasn't normal. How could I convince myself that everything was normal, except for this one misunderstanding, if I acted so abnormally? I wanted to reach in and grab my tray, but what if someone was watching? That would just be another chance for people to judge me.

I headed for the cafeteria exit and wondered when my best friend would notice I was gone.

I checked my phone for the billionth time. Earlier, I'd texted Kirsten—*u ok?*—then immediately regretted it. Obviously, she wasn't okay. And why did I write the message like I couldn't be bothered to spell out the full words?

I wanted so badly to talk with her, to be there for her—but maybe she didn't want to talk to me.

No, not maybe.

Definitely.

I looked at my phone one more time.

No messages. No texts.

THAT AFTERNOON, MY TEAM had a game against Eagle Creek. Coach Wight announced I was starting, then pulled me aside. "The great thing about sports," he said, "is that they take complete focus. While you're on the court, everything else that's going on in your life can just melt away. Do you know what I'm saying?"

I nodded.

Then I went out and scored 26 points. I hit threes and layups and everything in between. My height made it way easier to get shots off. My longer-legged speed made it way easier to take the ball to the hoop. The whole game was basically a dream come true.

Except I couldn't help feeling like the dream was at least one day past its expiration date.

When I got home, Dad was downstairs. He'd left the new *Dais* on the kitchen table, probably for me (or Mom? or both of us?) to see. The day's top headline:

"Coach Claims Misunderstanding."

I thought about going downstairs and telling him about my game. Maybe some good news would be helpful. Then again, maybe it would seem like rubbing it in.

Instead of going downstairs, I headed for the garage.

Grabbed a basketball.

I was already dribbling by the time I stepped onto the driveway.

I didn't even look at the hoop because that's not where I was going.

I was going to Kirsten's.

I was going to Kirsten's to tell her . . . what?

I didn't know.

More than anything, I was going to Kirsten's to listen.

Would she talk to me? She still hadn't texted me back, so there was no reason to think she would.

But I had to try. I had to do more than a three-letter text. I had to show her that I really did want to know if she was okay.

And if she could dribble to my house, I could dribble to hers.

That's what I kept telling myself as I jogged down the driveway, ball pattering against the pavement. I thought of all the times I'd watched her pushing her basketball in front of her, the ball bouncing in sync with her strides. I thought of Kirsten the last night I saw her, after she apologized to me, hurrying away.

Why didn't I follow her? Should I have followed her?

If I had, could we have cleared up this misunderstanding? (*So-called* misunderstanding?!) Her parents' letter to the editor came out the next day. Was that why she'd been so upset? Had she known her parents had written the letter? Or did they write it after she got home that night?

I made it to the end of our street and took a left onto the shoulder of the highway.

It was early February. I wore a hoodie but no coat. My breath gusted out of my mouth and nose. Exhaust billowed from tailpipes as cars whipped blurrily by. Their velocity jolted me.

How did Kirsten do it? How do you dribble with cars whirring on one side and a metal guard rail on the other?

The fact that my hands had gone numb from the cold didn't help. I could hardly feel the dimples on the basketball let alone keep control of it.

Speaking of the basketball. It hit a crack and sprang to my right. Instinctively, I lunged after it.

A horn blared. Tires screeched.

I must have gasped—gulped the cold air—because I coughed until my eyes went bleary.

It was only after the coughing, not to mention the thudding in my chest, calmed down that I realized I was still dribbling. In fact, the dribbling matched the thudding.

I'd just dribbled fifty yards, maybe a hundred, no sweat.

Well, that's not true. I was definitely sweating.

It may have been cold, but the combination of jogging behind a basketball for half a mile and almost getting flattened by oncoming traffic had gotten my sweat glands going pretty good.

My body had begun to warm up as I approached the exit. My hands had begun to hurt from the cold, but that was better than being numb.

Honestly, the pain felt kind of good.

Maybe it was the relief of escaping near death. In Health class we'd learned about beta- endorphins. They're the things that make runners go from feeling tired to feeling terrific in the middle of a race. Maybe they'd kicked in for me, too.

Whatever the reason, I felt as though I could dribble for days.

To tell the truth, dribbling while running suddenly felt easier than just running. It was like how bicyclists draft the riders ahead of them, making it easier to go faster. I was drafting the basketball . . . or something. I didn't know how to explain it, but I knew someone who could.

Kirsten.

It had always looked like she was somehow faster with the basketball than without it, and now, as I raced up the shoulder of the highway exit, I understood why.

And I couldn't wait to tell her.

We didn't have to talk about us, or about my dad, or about how she was doing—not if she didn't want to.

We could just talk about dribbling.

Highway dribbling, in particular.

I totally get it, I could tell her. And really, who else could say that? Who else could share that with her?

The town blocks swept by. I passed SunnySide, the local preschool. I passed Hadfield's, the local grocery store. I took a right here, a left there. A few times I looked down to make sure the ball was still there—that's how effortless the dribbling had become.

Only three and a half blocks from Kirsten's now.

I thought about how I could hear her dribbling up my driveway. Maybe she would hear me dribbling, too.

I thought about the beginning of the fall when she showed up at my front door for the first time. I'd thought she was showing up to see me.

Now I was showing up to see her.

Would that be okay?

I had almost convinced myself that it would when I got within a block of her house . . . and saw the cop car in her driveway.

I must've stopped moving my hand to dribble because there was my basketball, rolling down the slight incline of the street.

I tracked the ball down, scooped it up.

I stared at the cop car for a few seconds before turning to leave.

Instead of running, I walked. Instead of dribbling, I carried the basketball.

IT TURNED OUT THAT Dad's published denial didn't do much good. It didn't do much of anything. According to *The Dais*, and every other paper, he was still suspended--that was how the media and everyone else described his absence--"pending the results of the investigation."

Not only had the police parked at Kirsten's, but they showed up at my house, too. I'd just gotten off the bus when I saw the car backing out of my driveway. Had the other kids on the bus seen that? I was too busy running for my driveway to look.

"Dad?" I yelled as I entered the house. "Dad!"

I found him at the top of the stairs, on his way to the basement. "What is it, Mike? Are you okay?"

I was out of breath. "Cops," I said. "I just saw a cop car pulling out of—"

"It's fine, Mike. Just following protocol. Nothing to worry about."

Nothing to worry about? How could this be nothing

to worry about?

"Mr. Morris said something about a lawyer—"

"Standard procedure, Mike. That's all." Dad's voice was sharp, but he quickly softened it. "Really. It's nothing for you to worry about, okay?"

Which was it? Nothing to worry about? Or nothing for *me* to worry about?

I didn't get a chance to ask, though, because Dad had already closed the door behind him.

On page 6 of *The Dais*, there was a box score for the Rapid River girls' basketball team's latest loss. Kirsten hadn't played.

I felt like calling Eric and telling him the good news. "Kirsten's a Zero, Eric! Zero minutes played, zero points, zero assists, zero rebounds—*nothing but zeros*. You should totally email her and gain inspiration from her story!"

Dad wasn't even eating with us anymore. He just stayed downstairs, watching tape. Mom handed me a plate of tacos and said, "Bring these down to your father, okay?"

"I don't know if he'd like that," I said. Even after everything that had happened, it still seemed weird to enter the basement without permission.

"He has to eat, doesn't he?"

Maybe if you called him upstairs like usual, I

thought. But I didn't say that. Things were already tense enough between them; I didn't want to make it worse.

When I got downstairs, the TV was on.

"What are you watching?" I handed Dad the plate. He took it without taking his eyes off the screen.

"Game tape from the last game. Marshall brought it over."

Marshall was his assistant coach.

"Are you sure you should be watching that?" I asked. Wasn't that still sort of like coaching? What would Mr. Morris say? What would the cops say?

Dad turned to me. "What the hell else am I going to do, Michael? I have to be ready when this nonsense goes away."

He turned back to the game. I waited a few more seconds, just in case he wanted to say anything else to me. I wanted him to tell me that he had a plan in the works, just as he did when he gave away the girls' basketball jerseys, and when he put in the turnstile. My dad was a visionary—and once again I wanted him to share his vision with me. Then it could be *our* vision. We could watch it unfold in real life just as it had in our heads.

But Dad didn't say anything else—just kept watching the game tape—and after a while, I gave up and went back upstairs.

AFTER DAYS OF HARDLY TALKING to anyone, I suddenly couldn't shut up. But I didn't talk to Eric, or Mom, or Dad. And I definitely didn't talk to Kirsten.

Instead, I talked to my teammates.

Or, anyway, I talked *at* my teammates.

We had an away game at Groveland that afternoon, and I did all the normal talking—calling out screens, calling out offensive sets as I dribbled the ball up court, calling out plays as I inbounded the basketball, etc. But I didn't stop there. I followed teammates up the court and told them to step toward open spots on the court, or to pass the ball to the cutter, or to take a dribble to improve their angle before making an entry feed to the post.

When they turned the ball over, I yelled at them to get their head in the game as we ran back on defense.

When Coach Wight called a timeout toward the end of the second quarter, I interrupted him and pointed to the marker board he was holding. I told him that the play he had just drawn up wasn't going to work because

Groveland was in a zone defense. My finger dripped sweat on the marker board and I realized I had just talked over a coach. But I didn't care.

I didn't care because now that I had started talking I couldn't stop.

I didn't care because, unlike everything else that was going on in my life, I knew what to say. I knew the right words and terms and strategies. I knew how to fix what we were doing wrong.

All everybody else had to do was listen.

Which they didn't do. My teammates were silent the whole time I spoke, but they weren't listening. They couldn't have been. Because by halftime we were losing by 18 points. My teammates and I sat in Groveland's weight room—that's the room we were given for halftime—and waited for Coach to enter. (He liked to give us a chance to collect our thoughts before giving us his halftime speech.) Only I couldn't hold my tongue. I announced what each player was doing wrong, and what they needed to do differently if we wanted to get back in the game. As I lectured Nick Little—"If you understand what it means to cut someone off before they flash across the lane, why don't you do it?"—another voice finally cut in: "Lay off, Duncan."

I stopped talking and found the owner of the voice.

Adam Pilsner.

We were the only two standing.

"Is this all because you found out your girlfriend was giving you sloppy seconds after banging your dad?" he said.

Some players chuckled.

"If you ask me, the guy's always been a perv," Adam continued. "What were you telling me at lunch, Jake? That Mike's old man installed double mirrors in the girls' locker room just to spy on them while they changed?"

Jake Nichols sat next to Adam, and he didn't confirm or deny that he'd said these things during lunch.

"That's hilarious, Adam," I said.

"According to Nikki, he'd watch her stretch before gym class and like the whole time he had this humungo boner."

More laughter.

"Shut up," I said.

"You had your turn to speak. Now it's my turn," Adam said.

"No—now it's *my* turn." It was Coach Wight.

I didn't know how long he'd been there, but if he heard any of Adam's comments, he didn't say so. He just told us to take a seat with the rest of our team and then began his halftime pep talk.

This time, I didn't interrupt.

THE NEXT AFTERNOON, RUMORS of a televised interview spread quickly through the halls of the high school. Someone who arrived late in the day claimed that there were Channel 6 News mobiles lined up in the driveway and the street in front of Kirsten's house. *Did you hear? Did you hear about Kirsten?* someone would say, before somebody else—spotting me as I walked by—elbowed him or her into silence. *She's going to be on the 5 o'clock news!* he or she would finish, once they thought I was out of earshot.

When I got home after practice, I found Dad in the living room chair with the TV muted. I sat down on the couch next to him.

The five o'clock news started, and Dad turned up the volume. One of the news anchors gave a rundown of the show: the weather, sports, something about the President's international tour. "But first," she said, "a high school basketball coach has been accused of foul play with his star player—and we have an exclusive interview with the player and her parents."

They went to a commercial break.

"*Foul play*," Dad said, shaking his head but not taking his eyes off the TV. "They're making a sports pun out of real people's lives."

Just as they came back from the break, I heard the door to the garage open and close. *Mom*, I thought. Clips of newspaper articles flashed across the screen—first ones with headlines praising Kirsten ("Howard Scores 32 in Another Rapid River Win," "Krazy for Kirsten"), then the Letter to the Editor from Kirsten's mom and dad. The camera zoomed in to show the words "inappropriate relationship."

Suddenly we were in Kirsten's house, in her family's living room, with the three of them sitting together on a couch: Kirsten's dad, then Kirsten, then her mom.

Despite everything going on, it was a relief just to see Kirsten.

Still, she looked strange sitting there. She had her hair down instead of her usual ponytail and was wearing a noticeable amount of makeup, as well as a dressy green shirt with semi-sleeves. The shirt made her arms look awkward—too muscular or something. Her elbows were squeezed in by her parents' bodies.

The camera zoomed in so we couldn't see the interviewer. We could hear him, though. He read from the key parts of the letter and then asked questions.

Kirsten, would you characterize Coach Duncan's relationship with you as inappropriate?

"What do you mean by *characterize?*"

Her voice sounded strange, too—trembly and weak. *As far as you know, did Coach Duncan break the law in any way?*

"Not that I know of," she said. She swallowed hard. I'd never seen her so nervous and scared. She was looking away from the camera as she spoke as if checking to make sure she had the right answer. I thought about her on the basketball court, dribbling the ball as if it was on a string, her body moving around the court with total confidence.

Not that you know of?

Kirsten's dad put his hand on her shoulder. Which was all it took.

Just like that, the old Kirsten was back. She cleared her throat. She sat up and dislodged her elbows. She looked straight at the camera. "I mean, no. No, he didn't do anything illegal."

He didn't do anything that made you feel... compromised?

Kirsten again asked him to say what he meant by *compromised*, but this time she sounded almost annoyed. The reporter tried to clarify. He reused the phrase *inappropriately intimate*, as well as the words *physical* and *contact.*

"No," Kirsten said. "Nothing like that."

Thank God.

I mean, of course not.

But thank God anyway.

Then why do you think your parents wrote the letter to the paper?

Kirsten's Mom jumped in before Kirsten had a chance to answer: "We were just trying to protect our daughter," she said.

From what?

There was a pause. The interviewer clarified again.

Did she need to be protected from her coach?

Another pause. Mrs. Howard turned to her husband, who was looking at her, nodding at her to keep going. She turned back to the camera. "In retrospect, we may have overreacted."

In what way?

"The letter we wrote," Kirsten's dad said. "The language we used. That wasn't what we intended . . . ." he trailed off, cleared her throat, and said: "We probably never should have gone public—"

"He had no right, though—" her mother blurted out.

No right?

"Meeting with her all the time."

Kirsten nudged her mother with an elbow. "Mom," she said, "he's my *coach*."

"And we're your parents. He had no right," she said again, looking at the camera. "To take her away from her family. To take her out of school. To treat her like she was . . . like she wasn't just another teenager playing basketball for him. Like she was something *more*—"

Another elbow from Kirsten.

Something more? the interviewer asked.

Kirsten's mom opened her mouth but couldn't find the words.

Out of school? the interviewer pressed.

I thought about those passes he signed to let her shoot on our driveway.

"It wasn't just that. It wasn't just one thing. I'm sorry," her mom said—to Kirsten? To the camera? "I was angry. . . I was *so* angry about the whole situation." She paused. Now she was definitely talking to the camera again. "The words I chose—I didn't realize they were so . . . I didn't care . . . I didn't think about how they would sound to others."

What were you trying to accomplish with that letter?

When no one answered, the interviewer asked a different question: *What do you want to accomplish with this interview?*

Kirsten sat up more, freed her arms like she was clearing space for a rebound: "To play basketball," she said. "Just to play basketball."

So you won't be pressing any charges?

"That is correct," Kirsten's dad said.

I think Dad and I let out a sigh of relief simultaneously.

The interviewer tried to ask a few more questions, but with no success. Kirsten's Dad draped his arm across the couch and squeezed his wife's arm. "I think we've said all we wanted to say," he said.

"Amen to that," my father said. He clicked off the TV. "Now we can finally get back to real life."

He said it as though he'd been completely cleared—and he had, hadn't he?

We heard a thud and turned around. Mom stood in the kitchen next to two bulging bags of groceries.

She said, "There should be enough food in here, Jeff,

to last you and Mike a while." Then she turned and took a few steps towards the hallway.

"Where are you going?" Dad asked.

"To pack," she said.

"SAW THE INTERVIEW," ERIC said at lunch. He was beaming. "Must feel good to get that out of the way."

I didn't answer him.

"Now everything can go back to normal," he said, a huge smile still taking up half his face.

You'd think so, wouldn't you? I thought.

Not that I blamed him. Everything that had happened, it was a big misunderstanding, just as Dad had been saying all along. That's basically what Kristen's family had said, and that's what Dad tried to tell Mom last night. But she wouldn't listen to him. She said she didn't care what Kirsten said or didn't say. She said the time for clearing things up had expired a long time ago.

"The batting cage offer is still on the table," Eric said.

"I just want to rest, you know?"

After Mom finished packing, she'd come downstairs. Rather than argue more with Dad, she ignored him and put away the groceries. When she was done, she came over to the couch. "There should be enough food to last you a while," she repeated to me. "I even got you those fudge-covered granola bars you like so much, though if you ask me they're just glorified candy bars." I had absolutely no idea how to respond to that. *Granola bars, Mom? That's what you want to talk about?* Not that I had a chance to respond, anyway. Mom was already whipping around and picking up her suitcase as she announced, "I have to go." She looked at me one more time, opened her mouth to say something else, then changed her mind and headed for the door.

"I hear you," Eric said. "It's been a rough couple of weeks. You're still going to be at tryouts this weekend though, right?"

The question caught me off guard.

I said, "But it's only February . . . " then realized that that was the point: it was February.

High school baseball tryouts *always* take place on a weekend in mid-February. In the gym. After junior high, there are only two possible baseball teams to play on: JV or varsity. Up until sophomore year, there were at least half a dozen traveling teams to choose from—if you didn't make the Rapid River A team, you could still make the B team, and if you didn't make either team, you could still try to join A or B teams from the surrounding towns. Plus, ninth grade was the last year you could play in a no-cut league that had one practice and one game per week during the summer.

In tenth grade, you didn't have any of those options. You either made one of the high school teams or you didn't play organized baseball, and the early tryouts were a way to give whoever didn't make it a chance to get over it and go out for track or tennis instead. Later, once the snow melted, those players who aren't cut have a second tryout outside to determine who makes the varsity team and who plays JV.

Most of this had been explained to us in a letter during winter break.

"I can't believe I forgot about tryouts," I told Eric.

"You've had a lot on your mind," Eric said. "It's totally understandable."

For once, he said the exact right thing at the exact right time.

Then he wobbled, clutched the table.

"Are you sitting on your glove again?" I asked.

He shrugged, wobbled some more. "Gotta break this glove in by Saturday," he said.

AFTER PRACTICE, I SAT in the hallway across from the guys' locker room and waited for Dad to emerge. The glass doors leading in and out of the building were to my right. I watched the snow and ice dripping outside—off of cars and the building, onto the parking lot and the sidewalk.

It was the first non-freezing day in months.

The kind of day that was perfect for driveway basketball. For shooting outside without your hands freezing. For taking a missed shot out of the snowbank, dropping the snow-covered ball on the driveway, and watching it detonate against the asphalt, the snow melting almost as soon as it splattered.

Maybe when Dad came out I would challenge him to a quick game of one-on-one. We hadn't played since the last day of ninth grade. It was a tradition. He and I would play late into the night because we could: we didn't have school the next day. Mom would complain about not being able to sleep because of all the ball bouncing, but we knew she didn't mind. It may have been more sports, but it was also clearly father-son bonding time. Mom was the one who flipped on the floodlights.

Just like that, I was thinking about Mom again, and my brain scrambled to think of something else, to hold onto the good feeling of the sun shining through the glass.

"Hi, Mike."

I knew that voice. I turned my head back to the doors and there she was—or there her shadow was. I had to shield my eyes with my hand to make out her face.

"Hey, Kirsten."

And maybe it was the warm day, or the dripping snow, or the relief of getting to look at Kirsten instead of thinking of my mother, or the surprise of finally seeing Kirsten not just on TV but in real life—whatever the reason, after days of imagining getting to talk to her, of being angry at her for not texting or calling, of being angry at myself for being angry at her, of dreading that it would be different if we ever did talk again, of worrying that it would be tense, or awkward, or weird . . . after *all that*, here she was, right in front of me, and for some reason, none of that other stuff mattered. I felt totally calm.

Relaxed.

Even a little goofy.

I can't explain it, except to say I was too tired to think about reality.

"Is it really you?" I said. "The girl I spent all winter schooling in multiple sports?"

I think Kirsten was as surprised by my mood as I was. But she recovered quickly.

"Ummm. Sorry. Talk about awkward. You must have me confused with someone else. I'm the one who schooled *you*...."

"No, *I'm* the one who's sorry," I said. "I didn't realize—is today opposite day?"

"Let me check my calendar," she said, going to the wall and pretending to find the right date on an invisible calendar with her finger. "Nope."

"Which means it *is*," I said.

It was a lame joke, I knew—this whole conversation was completely stupid—but I didn't care. It had been a long time since I joked around with anyone, and it felt good.

"I'll kick your butt on opposite day, not-opposite day, or any other day," she said. She lightly kicked me on the side of my butt to demonstrate.

"Not in those shoes you won't," I said.

She was wearing brown leather shoes with a little bit of heel—not to mention snugly-fitting jeans.

"My mom got them for me," she said. "I almost asked her how she expected me to make a jump stop in these without traveling, but after everything . . ." I could almost see her swallow the rest of the sentence. She didn't want this moment to end any more than I did. "I'm sorry I haven't called or texted, or . . . I just didn't . . ."

She trailed off again.

"I get it," I said, trying to save the moment. "You were afraid I'd start beating you every time we played instead of just most of the time. Now that I'm healthy again, I mean. I don't blame you." She smiled, so I kept going. "I'll take you on right now, Howard. No more excuses."

That's when the locker room door started to open and Kirsten's smile disappeared: "I have to go."

The door closed and then began to open again.

"Mike—I'm sorry," Kirsten said. She had already backed her way partially out the door to the parking lot. "I'm not supposed to be alone with...." We both knew who she meant: she wasn't supposed to be alone with my dad—the man who was probably on the other side of the door. "I mean, my parents are probably here to pick me up. I should go. I'm sorry."

She pushed open the doors and hurried into the parking lot. Once again, Kirsten Howard had apologized to me while running away as fast as possible.

By then the locker room door was all the way open— and it wasn't Dad standing in the doorframe. It was Coach Wight. Or the back of him. He shuffled backward, dragging a full water cooler across the ground.

"Mr. Duncan," Coach said, looking over his shoulder, "is that you back there? Don't sweat it, Duncan: I don't need any help with this cooler. Thanks for asking, though."

I told him sorry and asked if he wanted me to bring the cooler somewhere.

"No problem," he said. "Like I said, I've got it. You looking for your dad?"

"Yes, sir."

He jerked a thumb over his shoulder. "He's still in the coaches' locker room. Go ahead and walk on back if you want. You might have to give him a good shake. He's pretty engrossed in there."

Coach held the door open for me. After the door had shut behind me, I tried to think through what had just happened. What was Kirsten talking about?

I'm not supposed to be alone with him.

If Dad was back to coaching, and she was back to playing, why couldn't she "be alone" with him? I don't mean *alone* alone—obviously, that would be a bad idea. But what about with me? Did what happened with Dad mean she could never hang out with me again? I remembered her text that night. (I'd only looked at it about a zillion times by now.)

Don't think I'll be going to your house anymore.

Dad was in the coaches' locker room, watching film. "Dad?"

"Oh, hey Mike." His head went back to the screen, then to a notepad on his lap. He jotted something down.

"You almost ready to go home?" I asked.

He kept writing in his notepad. "All of that nonsense started because I didn't realize it was dangerous to watch game film in my own home," he said. "I figure I might as well do it in public. If the athletic director or anyone else wants to put in the hours I do, they're welcome to watch with me."

I considered asking him about Kirsten or at least clarifying what he'd just said. Obviously, the problem hadn't been him watching film; it had been him watching film with Kirsten. But his voice sounded so bitter that I decided against pointing this out. More opinions about the Kirsten situation were the last thing he needed right now.

"I'm going to be a while," Dad said. "Do you mind taking the bus?"

"Sure," I said. "Hey, I was thinking, later tonight, maybe we could play one-on-one."

"Right now isn't a great time, Mike." His eyes were still glued to the TV. "These next few weeks are the most important of my career. If I ever want people to forget about . . . if I'm ever going to rehabilitate my image, I have to keep winning basketball games."

For the first time in a long time, Dad sounded certain of himself. Determined. He sounded like he had a plan. Okay, so it wasn't exactly a complicated plan. Everyone wants to win. But what everyone didn't know was how. I bet my dad already had tons of theories for, as he put it, "rehabilitating his image." And I was ready to help in any way I could.

"Want me to keep a shot chart or anything?" I asked him.

Dad didn't take his eyes off the screen. "Thanks, Mike. But I don't want you getting dragged into this."

I wanted to tell him that it was too late—I was dragged into this a long time ago. But if I said that it would sound like I was trying to guilt-trip him and he would be even less likely to tell me anything other than how sorry he was. So instead I just said, "Don't stay here too long, Dad. I mean, Kirsten already said you didn't do anything, so—"

He snorted. "Tell that to the people at the last game."

"Why? Did something happen?"

Dad paused the film and looked at me. He opened his mouth, then hesitated. "No," he finally said. "Not anything that you need to worry about."

Of all the reasons people had for refusing to talk to me last winter and spring, not wanting to worry me was the worst. It was like telling someone, "Don't look down." *Of course* that person's going to look down. *Of course* I was going to worry.

"Tell you what," Dad said. "How about we play a game of catch this weekend."

"Inside?" I said, even though I could tell by his smile that that's exactly what he meant. By *inside*, I meant *inside our house.* It had always been our favorite place to play catch, despite my mother's objections.

"Where else?" he said.

A game of indoor catch sounded great. In fact, it sounded perfect. Better than playing one-on-one, even. "I have baseball tryouts Saturday afternoon. Maybe we can play before that? That way I can get my arm warmed up."

"Deal," he said.

Dad gave me another smile, then turned back to the film. "Okay, Mike. I better get back to this," he said. "If there's one thing that will make the last few weeks go away, trust me—it's winning basketball games."

THAT SATURDAY, ERIC'S MOM drove us to the first day of the two-day tryouts. By the time we got there, the gym was already packed with players. Some were stretching, some were playing catch. There was equipment in the corners: bats, a tee, a hitting net. Three orange rubber bases had been placed on the court, with home plate directly below the raised basket on one baseline.

"Wanna play catch?" Eric said. Now that he had his coat off, I saw just how overdressed he was. While everyone else wore shorts and a t-shirt, he sported a pinstripe jersey with his name on the back, real baseball pants (the stretchy kind with a stripe down each leg), and those socks with the stirrups painted on. To make matters worse, every article of clothing was brand new. No holes. No stains. No fading from the sun. His shirt tucked snugly into his pants. It looked as if the entire outfit had been a single present—because it had been. He told me on the car ride over that his relatives in California sent all this stuff to him.

He tossed his softball into his glove over and over from close range as he waited for me to stand up. He had been using the softball to make the pocket of his glove as big as possible.

To say he looked nervous is an understatement of epic proportions. He could barely keep himself contained inside his crisply-ironed uniform.

"Sure," I told him, standing up. "But we probably don't want to play catch with your softball."

"Oh, right," he said. "Forgot about that."

He held the ball and stared at it as though he wasn't sure what to do next.

"Here," I told him, holding out my hand. He tossed me the ball and I put it between my boots before standing up.

As for me, I didn't feel nervous at all. Who cares about baseball tryouts when everything else in your life sucks?

Including your father.

Yeah, I knew he was going through a lot right now, but I couldn't help being a little annoyed with him. When I got up that morning I'd felt as good as I'd felt in weeks. No, things weren't back to normal. I didn't know when Mom was coming back, if ever, and I still had no idea what happened between Kirsten and my dad. But I couldn't help feeling excited to go to tryouts and even *more* excited about Dad's and my pre-planned game of indoor catch. I got up early enough to make breakfast for me and Dad. In fact, I'd made *his* specialty: frozen waffles with chocolate chips in each square. I'd even brought Dad his breakfast in bed. Or I'd tried to. He didn't answer when I knocked on his bedroom door. When I opened the door, he was nowhere to be seen. I finally found him downstairs watching more film. He thanked me for breakfast without even looking at the plate. Then he asked if I could carpool with someone else to tryouts.

Apparently, the game of inside-the-house catch had been postponed indefinitely.

Eric and I found a place next to some others playing catch. Eric backpedaled until he was about twenty feet away.

"Mind if we do some short toss first?" I said.

"Oh, right," he said again.

After he moved closer, I took the ball out of my glove and tossed it in his direction. I took it as a good sign that my arm didn't creak. Eric caught the ball and threw it back to me as if he was in a hurry. The ball was high and to my left, and I had to leap in the air to snare it.

"Dammit!" he muttered, kicking the wooden floor as though he was kicking dirt.

"Take it easy," I said. "We're just playing catch, Eric."

We threw the ball back and forth, gradually backing up until the whistle blew and everyone gathered in front of the coaches. After we signed in, the varsity head coach, Coach Wilson, split us all up into four groups and assigned each group a station in one of the four corners of the gym.

I started at the hitting net, where a coach sat on one knee next to a bucket of balls. He tossed each batter ten balls to hit into the net before the batter handed the bat to the next guy in line. As I waited for my turn, I spotted

Eric at the station to my left. He was doing a drill where he stood with his back to the wall and a coach hit balls at and around him. The goal was to stop as many as he could before they hit the wall.

And, I have to say, Eric *did* look better than when I last saw him. The movements he made with both his feet and his glove were more efficient than they used to be. He successfully stabbed his glove at a waist-level line drive and then lunged for a ball before it sunk below his knees.

By that point, his body weight was all leaning in one direction, though, and when the coach sent a ball behind him, Eric had no way to prevent it from smacking into the wall.

Eric slammed the wall, too—*intentionally*, with his glove—and yelled, "Move your feet, butthole!"

I'd never heard him call *himself* a butthole.

We moved in our groups from station to station, and every time Eric muffed a play he had a mini, and increasingly loud, tantrum. He threw his glove and stomped on it. He slapped his hip in frustration. He called himself every butt-related name he could think of.

Eventually, the guys in my group, mostly upperclassmen, took notice. They thought it was hilarious. "Is this kid for real?" one of them asked.

I don't think the guys in Eric's group knew *what* to think.

Maybe if I had been at the stations with him I could have done something about his behavior, gotten him to calm down. But I wasn't, so I couldn't.

Anyway, by the end of the session, I didn't want

anything to do with him.

The coaches told us to get some rest and they'd see us tomorrow—same time, same place.

Eric found me after I'd put my boots back on.

"How'd you do?" he asked me.

I told him I did fine.

"Me too," he said.

"What?"

"I think I did pretty well, too." He said it calmly, as though he'd really given it some thought. "I was counting the number of mistakes I made compared to the number of mistakes everyone else in my group made, and it was pretty close but I think I made less than most of the others."

"It's not all about mistakes," I said.

We started walking out of the gym and down the hallway.

"What's that supposed to mean?"

"Nothing. I just mean the coaches are probably looking at other stuff, too."

"What other stuff? This is a *tryout.* Nothing else should matter besides performance." His voice was getting heated.

We were out in the parking lot by then. "There's your mom," I said.

When I was fifteen feet from the car, I realized Eric wasn't walking with me. "Like what?" he said.

He was far enough away that he had to raise his voice.

"What?" I asked.

"Like what?" he said again. "What other things would they be looking for?"

"Forget it," I said. I moved toward him so I could lower my voice. "I just meant, you know, attitude and stuff like that."

"I'll work as hard or harder than anyone out there," he said.

"I know you will," I said.

"I'll practice all day if I have to."

"I know you will, Eric. That's not—that's not what I meant."

We were standing off to the side of the parking lot, almost out of the way of cars but not quite. Dane Bauer, the starting center fielder on the varsity team, had to swerve a little in his truck to get by. Eric's mom stuck her head out the window and said, "You boys coming?"

I looked at her and nodded my head—but Eric didn't budge. "What *did* you mean?" he said.

Another upperclassman drove by. He had to steer around us, too. Eric's Mom still had her head out the window.

"Nothing," I said. "I wasn't talking about you specifically—just generally." I took a few steps towards the car; when he didn't follow, I repeated, "I didn't mean you, okay?"

Finally, he said, "Okay" and followed me to the car.

Once we were on the road, Eric's Mom asked how it went, and Eric repeated what he told me: "Pretty well," he said. Then he told her about counting his and others' mistakes, and said, "So as long as these tryouts aren't rigged or something, I should be in pretty good shape."

As Eric's Mom drove me home, I wondered if Dad would be home. If he was, I'd ask again to play catch in our house. He and I used to play a lot. That was back when Mom traveled more frequently on business trips. One of us would stand by the front door, the other by the dinner table. The ball we used depended on the season—football, basketball, or baseball.

There was something satisfying about playing catch in the wrong setting. It's hard to explain, and it might sound a little cheesy, but I don't think Dad and I ever felt closer than when we tossed the ball back and forth, from the entryway to the dining room. It felt both rebellious and right—like we understood something in a way that most people couldn't. Most people being my mom, I guess, not that she ever found out about it. Maybe that's why I wanted to play inside-the-house catch so badly; doing so would make it easier to convince myself that things would soon turn back to normal. Any day now, I wanted to believe, Mom would return with her suitcase and start unpacking—just like she had when I was a kid.

We were only a block from my driveway when Eric's mom stopped the car. Which was odd. Why hadn't she turned into the driveway like she usually did?

Then I got my answer. I watched Dad's car back out of the driveway and pull up beside Eric's mom. Both of them rolled down their windows.

"Hi, Betsy," Dad said. "Thanks so much for carting Mike around today." She told him it was no problem at all. They stared at each other for a little while, then Dad said, "Well, I'm off to do some scouting." He thanked her again, rolled up his window, and drove away.

Eric's mom looked at me in the rearview mirror. "Do you want to have dinner at our house?" she asked me.

I told her thanks but no thanks.

SUNDAY'S TRYOUT BEGAN WITH more of the same. We were separated into groups and rotated from station to station, doing drills that tested our reflexes, our fundamentals. After that, we did some throwing. We played a game where our body parts were worth points. If a throw was caught above the waist, it was worth two points. If it was caught below the waist, it was worth one. The head had the biggest payoff: three points.

The first one to twenty-one was the winner.

I was paired with Paul Lindstrom, a senior pitcher. He was about my height, but bigger, with big cheeks and some stubble on his chin. As the two of us walked together to find a spot to throw, he said, "I've got a request."

I didn't say anything, but I looked at him to let him know I was listening.

"Any chance you'd be willing to get in a catcher's crouch when I throw? I haven't thrown a single pitch since we got here." He was swinging his right arm like a windmill as he talked. "I'll take fewer points or whatever—or better yet, maybe you can just call balls and strikes for me? We can tell the coaches you won the game if you want."

"Yeah," I said. "I guess so."

Why not? I didn't want to be at these tryouts anyway. That morning I'd once again had to ask Eric's mom to give me a ride.

"Thanks, man," Paul said. He tapped his glove to mine. "Stay right there."

As he moved away from me, he did his best to keep his strides in a straight line. His head nodded as he counted steps. A real pitcher's mound is sixty feet, six inches from home—and he was trying to get as close to that distance as possible.

As I got into a crouch, I couldn't help admiring Paul. In a gym where everyone else was trying to beat the guy across from them to impress the coaches, he just wanted to work on his game. Then again, Paul didn't need to worry about impressing the coaches. As one of Rapid River's best pitchers, his spot on the team was guaranteed. For him, this tryout wasn't a *tryout* at all. It was just practice, a chance to get ready for the upcoming season.

While everyone else made short-armed, floating throws in an attempt to make the ball go where they wanted it to, Paul threw from the wind-up, kicking his front leg high in the air and pushing off with the back leg. The ball got to my glove in a hurry and with a satisfying smack.

I not only called balls and strikes but started signaling different pitches: one finger down for the fastball, two for anything off-speed. Between pitches I hopped around the invisible plate, giving him different targets to throw to. I turned my hat backwards to look like an actual catcher.

When he had two balls and two strikes on an imaginary batter, I set up on the outside corner of the make-believe plate and mashed my glove into the hardwood. *Keep it low*, my glove was telling him.

He did. The ball landed in front of me and skidded under my glove. I hopped to my feet and chased after it.

When I got back, Paul was standing on the invisible plate. "Sorry about that," he said.

"No worries. That's right where I asked you to put it. No way the batter would've been able to lay off that pitch. If I was wearing pads, I would have stopped it." I held the ball out for him. "You wanna go against another batter?"

He put the glove under my hand, and I dropped the ball into it. "I like the way you think," he said. "What's your name again?"

"Mike."

"You got a last name?"

"Duncan."

"No way. You're Duncan's kid?"

I didn't know what to say to that.

"I mean, Coach Duncan." Then he said, "Listen— don't pay any attention to what all the other guys are saying. They're just immature assholes."

"What do you mean?"

What *did* he mean?

"About the chick lying for him—like I said, they're just being assholes."

The chick? Kirsten? *All the other guys?*

"QUIT CHEATING, BUTTLEAK!"

Paul and I turned to the voice, which I already knew was Eric's. He was four or five rows of players away from us. His face was rigid with rage.

Everyone stopped throwing.

"Get over it, kid," the guy across from him said. It was one of the players in my group from yesterday. "You missed."

"Like I missed the last one? And the one before it?"

"Just like that."

"I'm winning and you *know* it!"

"Jesus. Chill. What's this kid's deal?"

The guy, Brandon, looked around the gym for support.

"My *deal* is you're a lying butthole who needs to cheat to beat me!"

"That's enough, son," someone said.

It was the coach. The head coach. Coach Wilson.

But Eric didn't hear him. He was too consumed with rage. "It's either that or you can't do simple math!"

"Son—"

"Believe it or not, one plus one plus zero doesn't equal eight more points for you!"

"That's *ENOUGH*, I said!"

Eric turned to the coach, his face still angry, ready to shout at him, too, until he registered who he was looking at. His shoulders slumped instantly; his face faded.

"He… he was…" Eric stammered, "…he said—"

"Save it, son," Coach Wilson said. "Why don't you go walk it off? You can come back once you've cooled your jets a little."

Eric didn't move right away. He looked around the gym at everyone staring at him. When his eyes found me, I'm pretty sure they stopped. But I can't be sure because I wasn't looking at him anymore. I was looking at the hardwood floor. Staring at a seam between the wood panels.

By the time I raised my head, Eric was speed walking out of the gym.

Toward the end of tryouts, we ran around the orange rubber bases in the middle of the court. The coaches timed us. One at a time, we ran from home to first and first to third. While we waited in line, we cheered on the other runners—which seemed strange to me. It was hard to believe that everyone wanted everyone else to do well—the coaches were writing our times down on clipboards—but they probably figured that sportsmanship was part of the evaluation process.

We made megaphones out of our hands and shouted encouragement. We smacked the wood floor with open palms. A couple of guys put their fingers in their mouths and whistled. After someone had made it to third, he was greeted by congratulations and shoulder slaps.

After a while, it was my turn. Coach Wilson said, "Go!" and I heard the cheers as an afterthought. They were there— "Go Duncan!" "Book it, buddy!" "You got this!"—but they happened in the back of my mind, almost as if it was *me* who said the words. *C'mon, Duncan! Get a move on, man!*

As I approached second base I made an arc so that by the time I touched second I could run right at third.

Go, Duncan! Dig for it!

I ran through third and the coach told me my time. My first thought was: *That can't be right.* But then a bunch of guys came over and banged my shoulder. So I thought, *Maybe it is.*

Maybe I really did have the fastest time so far.

A few minutes later, Eric stepped up to home plate. I didn't know whether Coach Wilson gave him permission to return, or took pity on Eric. In any case, he let Eric take his turn.

Guys cheered him on the same way they cheered everyone else, but it somehow sounded different. Like they were mocking him. "You can do it, buddy!" "That's it!" It was as if they were talking to a pet. Even the whistles sounded condescending.

Eric was one of those guys who looked like he should be really fast but for some reason wasn't. It was as if his shoes had gunk on the bottom of them and he had to pry them off the floor with each stride. His arms seemed to be pumping faster than his legs.

My cheers were in my head and weren't really cheers so much as angry orders: *Go, dammit! Go faster! Pick up your legs and move!*

After he had rounded second and made it to third, he accepted the phony shoulder pats and w*ay to go's* and then took a seat with the rest of us to watch the remaining runners.

A few minutes later tryouts were officially over. The coaches thanked us for coming out and told us they had some tough decisions ahead of them. They said that a list of the players who made the team would be posted on the gym door by the next morning.

AFTER ERIC'S MOM DROPPED me off, I punched in the garage door code and waited for the door to open. When I did, I saw that there was only one car in the garage. As usual. What was unusual was that the car wasn't Dad's.

When I got inside I said, "Mom?"

"Mike? Is that you?"

She always said that. My whole life, anytime I yelled for her, she'd ask if it was me. Even though I'm an only child, so who else would be calling *Mom*? I usually found it annoying, but not this time. This time, it was music to my ears.

The voice came from the kitchen, and when I got there, there she was: my mother, standing at the counter, taking the lid off a wok. The food sizzled and crackled.

She wore the apron I made for her as a kid. "Stir fry's almost done. Just need to add the water chestnuts."

I didn't know what to say.

"You want to set the table, Mike?"

I watched my mother push the chicken and broccoli and carrots around the wok with a spatula and I wondered if this, her being here, was real—and if this was real, what about the last week?

All I said, though, was "Sure," and walked around my mother to the cupboard. I stared at the plates. "Is Dad eating with us?"

Pause.

"I asked him if you and I could be alone tonight."

I took two plates from the cupboard. "Why?"

"Why what, Michael?"

"Why did you ask for us to eat alone?"

Mom didn't answer right away. "Why don't we sit down first, okay?"

But I didn't feel like sitting down. "What's going on, Mom?"

She didn't answer me. She opened the wok again and dumped in the water chestnuts. She doused the stir fry with teriyaki sauce and the sizzling went up about ten decibels. "Please, Michael. Hand me those plates and I'll serve us up."

I didn't so much hand her the plates as she took them from me. Then she scooped some instant rice onto one of the plates, covered it with stir fry, and handed it to me.

"It's Sunday," I said. "Isn't it supposed to be chicken and rice today?"

She looked confused. "I suppose so. I guess I just thought—you like stir fry better, don't you?"

I nodded. "But what are you going to make tomorrow? Are Mondays still taco night?"

I knew the question sounded desperate. She hadn't said she was going to make anything tomorrow. Or even that she'd moved back home.

"Would you like me to come back tomorrow?" she asked.

That answered that question. She hadn't moved back in. If she had, she wouldn't have to *come back*. She'd already be here.

"Because I was thinking," she continued, "maybe you could come have dinner with me instead."

"What are you talking about?"

"Can we please sit down? Please?"

At first, I didn't budge. But finally I gave in.

Mom followed me to the table. After we were both seated I noticed her plate was still empty. "Aren't you going to have any?" I asked.

She looked at her empty plate and forced a laugh. "Oh. Right. Minor detail, huh?" Another forced laugh. "Oh, well. The truth is I've never really liked the stuff anyway."

I think the comment was her attempt at lightening the mood. By making a minor confession, she was trying to level with me about something that wasn't as serious as what we really needed to talk about. But the comment didn't lighten my mood.

It darkened it.

It made my mood pitch black.

"If you don't like it, then why did you make it?" I

asked.

"Oh, I don't know. When you have a culinary repertoire as small as mine, you stick with what works. You and your father always seemed to like it. Do you think it will make good leftovers? I can put it in some Tupper—"

"And that's supposed to make you some sort of great mother?" I said. "Making stir fry? Wow, Mom. You really suffered."

"I wasn't saying I suffered, Michael. I was—"

But I wasn't finished: "Is that what you told yourself when you decided to leave us? That you made stir fry even though you didn't like it?"

The speed and heat of my anger left me alert and light-headed at the same time. I stood up and stared down at Mom.

I waited for her to say something, to defend herself, but she didn't. I had silenced her.

I turned to go to my room.

"Make whatever food you want and eat it yourself," I said. I think I sideswiped the table with my hip as I walked out of the kitchen, but my adrenaline was pumping too hard to feel it.

I was sitting on my bed when Mom knocked on my door. I didn't answer, but she entered anyway.

She opened her mouth to speak, but I beat her to it. "Kirsten went on *TV*, Mom, and said Dad didn't do anything."

"Kirsten said what she needed to say, Michael. She did what she needed to do. That's what I'm doing too."

"What the hell is that supposed to mean, Mom?" I stood up. "You're saying you think Dad actually—"

"No—that's—I'm just saying—that's not what this is about."

"What is that supposed to mean? What the hell else could this be about?"

"I don't want you to have to choose a side, me or your father."

"Too bad. I did choose a side. I chose the side that didn't leave."

Mom was only a few feet from me now. Her hand was as shaky as her voice as she placed it on my shoulder.

I shrugged the hand away. "Get out of my room."

"I'm sorry, Michael."

"Get out,"I repeated.

"I didn't come here tonight to talk about . . . that. Any of that. I came here to tell you—"

"*Out!*"

The strength of my voice backed her up a few feet. She looked over her shoulder at the door, then back at me.

"I didn't leave you," she said. "I need you to hear me say that. This is not about you. We're a family. I know you're angry. But we're a family. I did not—I would *never*—leave you."

She stared at me for a while to make sure I was listening.

Then she left me.

ERIC WAS ALREADY THERE when I got to the gym door on Monday morning.

His eyes were red.

"Congratulations," he said. "You made it."

"Look, Eric—"

"I don't want to hear it."

"Okay. But—"

"But what? But I got screwed? Is that what?"

A group of guys who had also tried out came down the hallway toward us.

"Take it easy, Eric," I said.

"You take it easy!" he said. "That's what you did all year, and you still made the team!"

The guys stopped walking but didn't turn around to leave.

"That's not fair, Eric. I was—"

"I'll tell you what's not fair!" he said. He was tearing up. "Practicing for three hours a day, every day and still getting cut!"

"Sorry, man," one of the guys said. "When you suck you suck."

Eric yelled, "Screw you!"

His chest heaved in and out. The sobs erupted before his hands reached his face.

He collapsed to his knees.

Finally, after what felt like minutes, Eric stood up again. His heaving became deep breaths, then shallow, quick ones. He took his hands off his face and looked up at me. His eyes and the skin around them were soaked and puffy. He wiped his face with the back of his hand, which spread the wetness without removing it. What had been tears dripped from his earlobe.

Which wasn't the worst part.

In Eric's right nostril, there was a snot bubble--a snot bubble that shrank when he inhaled, expanded when he exhaled.

Some part of me knew that this was at least a little funny. Or that it could be. Just when life couldn't possibly get any worse, a snot bubble arrived and proved it could. Eric looked pathetic. But he also looked pathetically silly.

I should have laughed. If not in Eric's face, then at least inside.

But I couldn't.

I was too pissed.

Pissed at him for acting like this in public. Pissed at him for putting me in this situation. Even pissed *with* him because he was absolutely right. It *was* unfair. He *had* spent months practicing, while I barely had time to break in my glove. Baseball was his life and it was treating him like shit. It was unfair and Eric was right and I was pissed at him for being right.

That wasn't all that I was pissed about, of course. I was pissed that Eric could be right and so completely wrong at the same time. I was pissed that his unfairness was so much smaller than my unfairness. Once again I'd had athletic success and I couldn't enjoy it because the rest of my life was such a complete failure. All my life I'd wanted to be tall, and fast, and good—really, really good. And now I had a chance to be all those things, and I didn't give a damn.

So, yeah—I was pissed about a lot of things.

But mostly, I was pissed at that snot bubble. I *hated* that snot bubble. And I hated Eric for making it.

So instead of laughing, I tackled him.

I knocked him to the floor and pinned down his arms and the whole time I was screaming, "How could you not see this coming? What the hell is the matter with you? What did you think was going to happen? Huh? What the hell did you think was going to happen? How could you not have seen this coming?"

Then I reached back and punched the snot bubble right off his face.

I SPENT ALL MORNING expecting to be called into the principal's office. I had punched a kid, hard, and there was a bloody nose and witnesses to prove it.

I expected someone to enter whatever classroom I was in and ask me to come with them. Or for my name to be announced over the loudspeaker. Or for it to appear on the screens of our TVs in the hallways along with the rest of the day's announcements: *Today's Lunch: Sloppy Joes. Also, Michael Duncan beat his best friend to a pulp this morning.*

But none of this happened.

Which meant those two guys who watched me pummel Eric were assholes. How could they not turn me in? How could they see a kid lying bloodied on the floor and not seek justice on his behalf?

It also meant Eric hadn't turned me in. Which made him a lot of things. Stupid, mostly. I *deserved* to get in trouble. What the hell was he waiting for? For that matter, where the hell was he? I didn't see him in the halls or at lunch.

At some point it hit me: I could turn myself in. Of course. That's what I should do, and it's what I would do.

But not yet.

The next day, maybe.

First, I needed to get some answers. Well, I needed to get one answer. All this time I'd supported my dad. I hadn't pushed him. I hadn't pressed him for answers.

I'd believed him. I'd believed *in* him.

And I still did.

But something—*something*—happened between Kirsten and my father.

And before I confessed to my crime and officially put my crappy life in the law's hands, I was going to figure it out.

AFTER BASKETBALL PRACTICE, I hung around the gym and waited for the girls' varsity game to start. I sat in my regular spot, across from Kirsten's Krazies, just as the announcer began team introductions.

Except Kirsten's Krazies didn't exist anymore.

No guys had her name painted on their chests, or held up signs, or even cheered extra loud when the announcer called her name. If anything, she received *less* enthusiastic cheers than the other Rapid River starters.

Did the fans blame her in some way for what had happened? Was that what was going on?

Or were they somehow afraid to say or do anything— even something positive—in her presence?

Dad's name was the last one announced, and if anyone cheered for him, I couldn't hear them. The boos were too loud. Most of the booing came from Groveland's fans, especially their student section, but I was pretty sure some of the adults were from Rapid River.

This was the reception Kirsten and Dad got at *home* games. What did it sound like when they were away?

It was clear in the first few minutes that Groveland didn't have anyone tall enough to guard Janet Peterson, or good enough to guard Kirsten.

But the game stayed relatively close the entire first half—because Kirsten allowed it to.

It wasn't that she played badly. She wasn't lazy on defense or careless with the ball on offense. When she was open for a shot, she took it. But Groveland's strategy was to keep the ball out of her hands. They put two girls on her after every made basket to force somebody else to bring the ball up the court and start the offense. As Kirsten ran through screens, Groveland's girls immediately switched who they were guarding so the screens didn't work.

Kirsten wasn't doing anything *wrong* out there. You couldn't call the score at the half, 22-22, her fault. Groveland was determined to make someone other than Kirsten beat them, and so far no one else had been able to do it. Despite Janet's size advantage, she missed one short-range shot after another. Probably because she felt so out of sync. Without Kirsten running the point, the first half never gained much of a flow.

And while it wouldn't be fair to blame Kirsten for that lack of flow, there was no question in my mind that she had allowed it to happen. Because while on paper Groveland's strategy sounded good—keep the ball out of Kirsten's hands—it should have never worked. Not against someone as good as Kirsten.

Two girls guarding Kirsten? Get her the ball anyway. She can dribble around or through them, race up the court and play 5-on-3 basketball.

Switching on every screen? Get her the ball then, too. She could take advantage of whatever mismatch presented itself. If she ended up with a center defending her, Janet probably had a guard on her, and it would have been Kirsten's choice whether to go one-on-one herself or pass to Janet in the post.

None of this could happen, though, if Kirsten didn't demand the ball.

Which is exactly what she did in the second half.

Whether stealing the ball from her opponent or catching close-range passes from her teammates, Kirsten spent most of the second half with the ball in her hands, racing up the floor, setting up her teammates with layup after layup. Once Rapid River made a few shots in a row, it was as if no one on the team could miss. Kirsten's teammates nailed shots from all over the floor—from the corner, from the elbow, from beyond the arc.

Groveland took a few timeouts in an attempt to stop Rapid River's momentum, but it didn't work. The shots kept going in, and by now all the Rapid River girls were high fiving as they ran down the court.

Except for Kirsten. She didn't have time to celebrate. She was too busy pouncing for another steal.

With six minutes left the lead was big enough, 64-32, that Dad took out all five starters to a nice ovation and brought in the reserves. He high fived each player as they ran past him to the bench, including Kirsten.

Rapid River was given another ovation when the final buzzer sounded.

I sat in the hallway and watched the Rapid River players empty out of the locker room.

Finally, Kirsten shuffled out.

As usual, she was the last one to leave. This time, though, no one else waited with me to get an autograph or say congratulations.

She was wearing nice clothes again. Jeans, brown boots, a black coat with buttons. As the door closed behind her, she wrapped a white scarf around her neck.

She spotted me right away. "Hey, Mike."

It was so weird: once again it had felt like she'd been avoiding me, like she didn't want to see me, like I might never talk to her again. But now that she was there in front of me, she didn't look disappointed or reluctant to talk. She marched right up to me.

"Good game," I said.

She shrugged. "The second half was okay."

"Yeah, what was up with that first half?"

It sounded like I was criticizing her, but I didn't mean it that way, and that's not how she took it.

"I don't know," she said. She pivoted so her back was to the wall, then slid down until she was sitting next to me on the floor. "The truth is . . . the truth is I'm ready for the season to be over."

She said it as though it was a dark, dirty secret.

"THE Kirsten Howard?" I said. "Sick of basketball?"

"I thought everything would go back to normal after going on TV, you know?" she said.

Man, did I ever.

"But it didn't," she said. "Things are different. It all feels . . . different."

She looked different. And not just because of the nice clothes. Kirsten was clearly wiped out. She actually had her eyes closed, almost as if she was going to take a nap right there and then.

When she opened them, she asked, "Is that why you wanted to see me? To give me a hard time about my crappy play in the first half?"

"No," I admitted.

Some headlights shined through the glass doors, then shut off. "That would be my dad," Kirsten said.

"Oh," I said. "This can wait."

Of course, it couldn't wait. At least I hadn't thought so until right now. But seeing her like this, so completely drained—I changed my mind.

"So can my dad," she said.

I looked out the glass doors, but it was too dark to see anything. I wondered if her dad could see us.

I took a deep breath. Now or never. "What happened between you and my dad?"

"What do you mean?" she said. Her voice instantly changed pitch. She didn't like the question.

"I mean—"

"Did he hit on me?" she said. "Is that what you're

asking? Did he stick his tongue down my throat? Did he try to bone me?"

"Jesus."

"Well? That's what you want to know, right? Everyone else does."

Who was everyone? Had jackass guys like Adam Pilsner said these things right to her face? Had girls said these things, too?

Kirsten stood up. She wanted to leave, and I didn't blame her. But I also needed to know.

I stood up next to her. "Well, yes. I mean—"

"I already answered that question," Kirsten said. "On *TV*." Her hands were fists and she pounded me on the chest with them. "Do I really have to answer it again? For *you*? You know us, Mike. You were there the whole time. *Of course* nothing happened. How could you think that we... how could you think that *I*..."

"I wasn't blaming *you*," I said. "I just—"

She started pounding my chest again.

"No, Mike. For the last time—*no*. Nothing happened. Okay? Are you satisfied?"

When I didn't respond, she turned to leave.

"No," I finally said. "I'm sorry, but no—that's not enough. There has to be something . . . something else. There has to be. One second you're in my life and everything's fine, and the next you're running away like you are now. Are you telling me my entire life fell apart for no reason?"

At long last, it was my turn to do the sobbing.

"I know I should be asking my Dad. I know I have no

right to ask you. But please. *Please.* I need to know."

Full-body spasms bent me in two.

Kirsten kneeled next to me, but didn't say anything. When the spasms stopped, I said, "I am so sorry to ask you these questions," I said again. "I *am*. But if there's anything you can tell me . . ."

I let my voice trail off.

Kirsten thought about it for a few moments. When she spoke, her voice was soft: "He told me he was going to get a divorce," she said. "Okay? The night I stormed off. He told me he was going to divorce your mom."

She stopped talking for a moment, her head tilting, her eyes scrunching. She was analyzing my face, trying to see whether I was okay. Then she opened her mouth to talk some more, but I interrupted.

"When?"

"What?" she asked.

"When was he going to get the divorce?"

Kirsten grimaced. This was painful for her. "I don't know, Mike. He didn't give a specific date. Soon, though. That's what it felt like. I don't know."

She kept going: "There we were watching film like always, and then suddenly he was telling me how badly your mom treated him, how she didn't understand him and never would. How he couldn't take it anymore. I didn't say anything. His voice got emotional, and I got overwhelmed. I told him I had to go. That's when he told me not to tell you—to let him figure out how and when to do it. I said I had to go again, and I did. I left. That's how you saw me when I got outside and that's how my parents saw me when I got home. When I explained what had happened, my mom was furious. They both were. At what he said that night, and at the rest of it too. The passes out of study hall. Encouraging me to skip the family trip to Florida. I didn't have the energy that night to tell them *again* that I did those things too, not just Coach Duncan. Especially since they would have just said it didn't matter; Coach Duncan was the adult. But also because I was mad at him too. He *is* an adult, Mike; he *shouldn't* have told me that stuff about him and your mom. He definitely shouldn't have told me not to tell you. Mom wrote the letter that night."

Kirsten took a deep breath. "She overreacted—even *she* gets that. But it was my fault. If I saw my daughter like that, I would have overreacted, too. None of this would have happened if I hadn't gotten so upset. I'm so sorry."

"Yes, it would have," I said it out loud but I meant it for myself.

"What?"

"Not the stuff that happened between you, but . . . My mom left my dad the day you were on TV. . ."

I didn't need to finish the sentence. Kirsten's eyes had already widened with sympathy. "I'm sorry, Mike. I didn't know. I'm so, so sorry."

"It's not your fault," I said. Because it wasn't. Of course it wasn't. "Dad should have never done that. He should have never said those things to you."

He should have said them to me, I thought, *or to Mom. He should have said them to the people he was planning to leave. The people he promised he would never leave. Not to you. Never to you.*

"It's his fault," I told her. *I had asked him, point-blank, if there was anything to worry about—and he lied. I blamed Mom for leaving when he had already decided to ditch us. He kept me in the dark, but he had no problem sharing his actual thoughts and feelings with one of his basketball players—with my girlfriend.*

"Where are you going, Mike?"

Until she said it, I didn't even realize that I was on the move.

"I'm sorry," I said over my shoulder. "I need to think. I need to go."

AT SOME POINT IT dawned on me that I had just done the same thing to Kirsten that she had done to me that night on the driveway: apologized while fleeing the scene. Where I was fleeing to, I had no idea. I just knew I had to go . . . somewhere. So long as I kept going, it didn't matter where I ended up.

Maybe Kirsten had felt the same way that night Dad told her his plans to divorce Mom. Maybe she didn't know she was heading home until she burst through the front door and saw her parents' concerned faces. Anyway, that's how I felt. One second I was speed walking away from the school, from Kirsten, from what Kirsten had just told me; the next I was arriving at the other school parking lot, the one with the sports fields next to it. I didn't know why I'd ended up there—not at first. I'd been on automatic pilot.

But now that I was there, I knew it was the right place to be. If I wanted to keep moving, where better to do so than a sports field?

Maybe somewhere deep down Kirsten had needed

to see her parents that night. Maybe, despite the letter and the controversy it started, her dad and even her mom had given her exactly what she needed that night. I hoped so.

What I needed was to run. At that moment, it felt like it was all I had left. Every good thing that had happened that year had turned bad, with little hope of getting better. Except for my leg. My leg had been badly busted, but now was healed.

Everything else in my life felt like it was long gone. I'd never felt more abandoned. More betrayed.

I'm not going anywhere, he'd said.

All this time, I thought sports weren't a choice, not for someone like him.

Not for someone like me.

No, it was more than that. I thought Dad *had* made a choice. I thought we both had. By choosing sports, I thought we were choosing each other.

But I was wrong.

Maybe for the first time, I wished my dad wasn't Coach Duncan; I wished he was a regular guy, with regular priorities. I wished he was the kind of dad who didn't think twice about driving his hurt kid to the hospital.

I neared the football field and thought about running on it. Racing from one end to the other. Recreating my last play, minus the helmet to my knee cap.

No—on second thought, I didn't want to edit out my injury. If I hadn't gotten injured, I might not have ever started hanging out with Kirsten. And as bad as things had gotten, I didn't, wouldn't, couldn't regret *that.*

The baseball field then. I could run around the bases, just as I had during tryouts. Only this time I'd be aware of how fast I was moving.

I entered the diamond and stepped into the batter's box. I pretended to tap an invisible bat against home plate. I looked up at the mound, ready to face an imaginary pitcher.

It was only then that I realized the mound wasn't empty.

The person was hunched over, on their knees. He or she raised their arm in the air. Something glimmered for a moment in the moonlight.

"C'mon, you Buttcrust," a voice said.

"Eric?" I said.

"MIKE?"

"Who are you talking to?"

"Nobody."

"Who's the Buttcrust?"

"This mound. It's frozen solid."

I walked toward the mound. "What are you doing?"

"Trying to conduct a burial service." When I got a few feet away, I saw what was in his hand: one of his mom's little gardening shovels.

"What are you burying?"

He set down the little shovel and held up the *Baseball Encyclopedia.*

I wanted to ask him what he was doing burying a book in a pitcher's mound, but he spoke first.

"I'm sorry, Mikey."

Wait. What? *He* was sorry? What did he have to be sorry about?

"I just couldn't see it," he said. "I wanted it… to make the team, to get an at-bat, to… I wanted it so badly, I couldn't see how impossible it was. You tried to tell me, and I couldn't hear you."

I was about to say *I'm sorry, too,* but the words seemed inadequate, especially as a response to his apology. Echoing his words weren't nearly good enough.

"I'm not sure it's wise to bury the Bible," I said instead. "The baseball gods might smite you or something."

"I'm willing to risk it. What are you doing here, anyway?"

I told him.

Everything.

I started with Kirsten running down the driveway and worked my way forward. Eric didn't interrupt, analyze, or judge. He just listened. Even in the pitch-black, I could tell he was listening closely and completely.

As I told him about the game I'd just watched, how wiped out Kirsten had looked, I felt my anger rising once more. It occurred to me that Dad had been right: winning solved a lot of problems. In just one game, fans had gone from booing to cheering. And if his team kept winning, the cheering would no doubt keep getting louder. Dad would come out of this fine. But how about everyone else? Kirsten Howard, THE Kirsten Howard, didn't want to play basketball anymore, and it was his fault.

Dad may have been a visionary—but how many people would he hurt so he could make his vision a reality?

Which got me thinking about a freezing cold day at

the beginning of winter, when Mom was in the car, staring at this very field.

"So," Eric said, "what are you going to do now?"

Just like that, I had come up with an idea and made up my mind to act on it. I pointed toward the backstop.

No, I pointed *through* the backstop, toward the football field.

"I'm going to steal that turnstile," I said.

IN ALL THIS DARKNESS, Dad's turnstile was bathed in light. The bulb, fastened to the equipment shed, beamed down on the turnstile like a spotlight.

Had Dad put the light there himself? I wouldn't put it past him.

"I bet he didn't even ask for permission before putting this in," I said to myself but out loud. "I bet he didn't care what other people thought of the idea."

"I'm not sure this is one of *your* best ideas, Mikey."

I didn't look at Eric. I couldn't bear to. A few minutes earlier, when we'd first gotten in the light, I got my first glimpse of what I'd done to his face. He had a bad shiner under his eye and a cut by his cheekbone. "I told you, Eric—I'm not expecting you to help."

I locked my fingers on the chain-link fence next to the turnstile and got ready to climb.

"So you're going to drag this thing all the way to your house on your own?" Eric asked.

I was at the top of the fence, reaching for the

turnstile. "I'll figure it out."

I lifted the turnstile a few inches.

"I just don't think you've thought this one through, Mikey." His voice was gentle like he was a negotiator talking me off a ledge.

"What the heck are you doing up there?"

It was a different voice.

I turned my head. "Kirsten? I thought your dad picked you up."

"He did. I snuck out of the house. Just because I don't text you back doesn't mean you get to do the same to me."

I felt my pockets for my phone. Nothing. Must have left it in my gym locker.

"Are you going to answer my question?" she asked me.

When I didn't respond right away, she pivoted around: "Hey, Eric."

"Hey."

"What the heck is Mike doing up there?"

"Stealing that . . . that . . . what's that thing called again, Mikey?"

"A turnstile."

"Right. He's stealing that turnstile and bringing it to his house."

"That doesn't sound like a very good idea," Kirsten said.

"That's what I told him," Eric said.

I slid the turnstile higher up.

"Why would he do that?" Kirsten asked.

"To get back at his dad, he said."

"Yeah, that definitely sounds like a bad idea."

"No argument here."

I slid the turnstile the rest of the way off the pole, then pushed it away from Eric and Kirsten. It crashed to the ground.

"How is he going to carry the turnstile to his house?"

"I already asked him that," Eric said. "He said he'd figure out a way."

"What is that supposed to mean?"

"It means," I said, jumping off the fence and landing on the ground, "that you don't need to worry about it. Seriously, you should go home. This is something I need to do, okay? But it's not something you two should risk getting in trouble for."

"No doubt about it," Kirsten said. "This is a really stupid idea."

"Preaching to the choir," Eric said.

"Any chance we can talk him out of it?" Kirsten asked.

"Don't think so," Eric said.

"That's what I thought," Kirsten said.

She grabbed an end of the turnstile.

So did Eric.

WE WALKED DOWN THE street, carrying the turnstile. Kirsten asked Eric what happened to his eye. "Ask our fearless leader," Eric said.

There was a brief silence as we passed the town hospital, and I wondered if I was supposed to fill the silence with a confession. *What happened to Eric's face? My fist happened to Eric's face.*

But Kirsten had already moved on to another question: "What are we going to do once we get this to his house?"

Truthfully, I didn't know for sure. Either bring it inside and shove it down the staircase to the basement or—if we couldn't get the turnstile through the door—just leave it on the driveway. I started to tell Kirsten this, but she said, "I wasn't talking to you. I was talking to Eric. It doesn't do any good talking to you since you're clearly not thinking straight."

"Agreed," Eric said.

The three of us were positioned along the turnstile—Kirsten in front, me in the middle, Eric in back. We passed the park and took a right. In two blocks, we'd reach the Big Scoop ice cream shop. From there it was only a few more blocks to the highway.

"Did Mike even tell you how this was supposed to get revenge on his dad?" Kirsten asked.

"I just need him to see that—"

"Mike. Do you mind? I'm trying to talk to Eric."

"As you said," Eric answered, "Mike isn't thinking clearly, but I'm pretty sure this is meant to be symbolic."

"Exactly," I said.

"What does that even mean? A symbol of what?" Kirsten asked.

"Beats me," Eric said.

"I didn't ask you two to come," I reminded them. "I told you *not* to come."

We passed Big Scoop and took a left.

We could see the exit ramp from here.

But that was as close to the highway as we got.

I saw the lights before I heard the siren.

"Hey, Eric," Kirsten said, "Think there's any chance that that's a symbolic police car, not an actual one?"

THERE WE SAT, ROTTING behind bars in a jail cell, waiting to be granted our one and only phone call, which would likely be our last-ever connection to the real world.

Okay, that's a bit of an exaggeration.

Okay, that's a *humongous* exaggeration.

Truthfully, we sat—just the three of us—at a table in a carpeted room with two windows and no bars.

We'd been sitting there for almost thirty minutes.

When we were first brought in here, a cop—not the one who arrested us—sat down, dropped a big yellow notepad on the table, and, after introducing himself (Officer Borg), asked us what happened.

At first, I thought this might be a strategy. Good cop, bad cop. Pretty soon, I thought, the bad, insane cop would come in and work us over. The only light would be a lamp shining down directly on us.

But that didn't happen. It was just the one cop, who wasn't exactly nice but wasn't menacing, either. The lights stayed on the whole time. There wasn't even a lamp in the room.

Officer Borg just blinked a lot and let us talk.

And we *did* talk. Or I did, anyway. I told him I had stolen the turnstile and how I'd stolen it. I told him about climbing the fence and pulling up the turnstile and pushing it over and carrying it through the streets. I described our exact route. I even started to tell him why I stole it. But it turned out that Officer Borg was as unimpressed with symbols as Eric and Kirsten.

"Okay, son, that's plenty," he said, flipping his notebook closed.

After he left the room, I said, "For what it's worth, I'm sorry I got you both into this."

"You better be," Eric said. By how he said it, though, I could tell he wasn't angry.

"If this ends up meaning I can't play ball," Kirsten said, "I'll kick your butt." She blew a strand of hair away from her mouth.

"Why don't you sound more concerned?"

"Something tells me we'll be fine," Kirsten said. She nudged me with an elbow. "No thanks to you."

"Fine?" I asked. "What makes you say that?"

She smiled. "There have to be some advantages to being a star athlete, right?"

A few minutes later, our parents arrived.

All six of them.

Together.

We watched them move as a group to a row of chairs to the right of our "cell." Then they moved to the waiting area outside our window. Their chairs faced a different direction, so they didn't see us as they sat down.

My dad sat in the middle, holding a clipboard. The others leaned in and watched him fill out a form. My mother, who sat next to Dad, pointed to the form and said something. Dad nodded his head.

I was still pissed at him. No, not just pissed. A part of me was seething. What he did—the things he told Kirsten, the things he didn't tell me or Mom—it was going to take a long time to forgive him. Maybe I never would.

But it was weird. Even as I knew I wasn't done being pissed at Dad, even as I understood that I was currently sitting in the clink because of my half-baked plan to get back at him in the only way I could think of, even as I believed that a lot of this was his fault—even after all that, I was still glad to see him there.

Go figure.

Maybe it had something to do with all the other people who were there, too.

Gazing out at them, I realized that this was the first time I had ever seen them in the same room together. As far as I knew, my mom and dad had ever interacted with Kirsten's mom and dad. After all the stuff that had happened because of decisions and choices they made, this was the first time they'd actually had to face each other.

If it was uncomfortable for them, good.

Okay, so maybe that was partly why I was glad to see

them. Maybe I just wanted to see them suffer.

Maybe.

But it wasn't the only reason.

As I watched them lean toward one another, I couldn't help thinking that it was kind of great. Bailing your kids out of jail wasn't the best circumstance to meet, I'll grant you that—but I'd take what I could get. Especially since, surprisingly, they weren't fighting with one another. They weren't at each other's throats. Just the opposite. They were working together to take care of the problem.

As I thought about all this, I got up and reached for the door handle. It was unlocked. (Really, in retrospect, this was the most pitiful jail cell ever.)

Stepping into the waiting area, I said, "Hey, Mr. and Mrs. Pendleton. Hey, Mr. and Mrs. Howard. Hey, Mom and Dad. I'm glad you guys could all make it."

Behind me, I heard Eric and Kirsten agree that I was certifiably nuts.

SUMMER SEASON

I'M STANDING ON THIRD base, trying to decide whether or not to do it.

Whether or not to steal home.

It's June: the last JV baseball game of the season. We're down to the last inning, and the game is tied (4-4). There are two outs.

I look up in the stands behind the chain-link backstop and spot Eric and Kirsten. Eric's reading his *Baseball Encyclopedia*. He's decided not to bury the book after all. I'm glad. I wouldn't even mind helping him find more Zeros. The more I think about it, the more I get Eric's interest in their stories. Zeros are numbers too, if that makes sense.

The pitcher goes into his windup and throws a fastball that the ump calls high. I've taken a good lead, but I trot back to the base between pitches.

I watch the pitcher nod at whatever sign the catcher gave him, lean back, show me the back of his jersey as he twists and kicks and throws. The pitch is low.

I look up at the stands again. Eric's watching me. I wonder if he's thinking what I'm thinking.

If I'm going to steal home, now is the time to do it.

The pitcher is a lefty, which means his back is to me when he throws. He's pitching from the windup, which means I'll have more time to get a running start. And the batter, Brett Jefferson, is a righty, which means the catcher is less likely to see me coming.

I let the pitcher throw another pitch. Swing and a miss. Strike one.

Mom is in the stands, too. She's been coming all season. Dad's also there—but on the opposite end of the bleachers. Ever since the turnstile incident, Mom has been living in the house again. It's Dad who moved out. I haven't visited his apartment yet. I don't think he spends much time there, anyway. He's usually in his office when I get to the locker room for practice and is still there watching some game or other as I change back into my school clothes to go home. I don't ever join him, but I do stick around sometimes. I have an app on my phone that allows me to watch pretty much any sporting event, and sometimes I'll guess what I think Dad must be watching and, sitting on the bench by my locker, we'll see the same game, not together but close enough. I asked Eric if that was weird and he said it wasn't. "Then again," he reminded me, "I once tried to bury a book, so I could be wrong about that."

The pitcher throws a low and away slider that bounces in the dirt before the catcher stops it. Amazingly, Brett, who leads our team in strikeouts, checks his swing.

If I'm going to steal home, that would have been a good pitch to do it.

Kirsten is sitting next to Eric, in the front row of the bleachers. She has a baseball hat on, and she's covering the brim with her hands, shielding her eyes from the sun. After her season ended in the section finals, she decided to take a couple-month break from basketball. She's come to almost all of my games and as a result, her cheeks are slightly sunburned. A few weeks ago, as I walked her home, she grabbed my hand and held it the rest of the way to her house. She still hasn't been back to my house but just yesterday she got on her tip-toes and gave me a peck on the mouth.

She's tilting her head now, listening to Eric tell her something.

Time is called on the field. The catcher, the coach, and the third baseman gather around the pitcher as they talk strategy. It's a 3-1 count, so they have to decide whether to go after the batter or pitch around him and risk a walk.

Eric's been to almost every game, too. Afterward, Kirsten likes to tell me what new statistic or fact she learned from him. "That guy doesn't need a *Baseball Encyclopedia*, Mike," she says. "He's a *human* encyclopedia."

It's at this moment—as the catcher and the third baseman trot back to their positions, as the coach walks back into the dugout, as Kirsten nods her head at whatever Eric's saying—that I decide to do it.

I'm going to steal home.

I'm going to steal home because it's the ideal

situation to do it.

I'm going to steal home because Brett isn't much of a hitter, and there are two outs, and this may be our best chance to win the game.

I'm going to steal home because this is the last game of the season and therefore my last chance to do it.

I'm going to steal home because it will give the three of us—Kirsten, Eric and me—something to talk about. This is the kind of play Eric loves, one that shows up in an obscure statistic you can only find if you look hard enough. There was a time, he told me once, when stealing home wasn't all that uncommon. Hall of Famer Ty Cobb did it eight times in one season and fifty times in his career. But now it's almost unheard of. Probably the most exciting play in all of baseball, and no fan ever thinks about it anymore, because no player has the guts to attempt it. "Doesn't that seem sad?" Eric asked me. I agreed that it did.

Mostly, though, I'm going to steal home because there are people behind the backstop who will watch and wait and root for me whether I make it safely or not.

I glance once more at the stands. Both Kirsten and Eric are looking at me. They've turned their attention away from the pitcher and batter as if they know what's about to happen. I glance at Dad and wonder if we're thinking the same thing. I look at Mom and—okay, there's no way she has a clue what I'm planning to do, but she's watching me intently, and I have to give her credit for that. I take a few steps off third base, wait for the pitcher to start his motion, and I'm off, racing for home and whatever's going to happen when I get there

ACKNOWLEDGMENTS

It took one daydream to come up with the characters and general plot of this book and less than two weeks to write the first 100 pages of the first draft. (I wish I could say the same about anything else I've ever written. This book remains my only case of lightning-struck inspiration.) That was in 2008. I've been writing and re-writing the book ever since. The manuscript got me my graduate degree, my first agent, and a date with my now-wife. What it didn't get was published. After years of close calls and near misses, I had to deal with the reality that my favorite thing I've ever written might never become an actual book.

The fact that you're holding this copy means I have a lot of people to thank and not enough space to do it.

To the mentors and students at the University of Minnesota's Master of Fine Arts Program: Thank you for helping me shape and then re-shape the original manuscript, and for giving me three paid years to do so. To my brother, Andy Hueller: As identical twins and YA authors, we're like the Coco and Kelly Miller of Minnesota publishing. To everyone with whom I grew up talking stats and trading cards and playing sports: Hopefully you recognize us in this book. To my wife, Mari, also a writer and the kickassiest of editors: Words ain't enough. Almost a decade later and we're still playing for keeps,

Kesselring. And lastly, endless gratitude to INtense Publications: Like I said, this is my favorite thing I've ever written. Hopefully, our readers love it too.

ABOUT THE AUTHOR

Patrick Hueller lives, writes, and teaches in Minnesota. He has an MFA in creative writing from the University of Minnesota. Over the last several years, he has published a handful of critically acclaimed YA novels under the pen name Paul Hoblin: *Foul*, a sports-horror book, was described by Booklist as "unbearably tense"; *The Beast* was a Junior Library Guild selection; *Archenemy* made ALA's Rainbow List. Under his own name he published *Stu Stories: The Adventures of Dirt Clod and His Sidekick Bird Bones* (Cedar Fort, 2017)—a collection of humorous larger-than-life tales for middle schoolers.

Learn more about Patrick and his books at
www.patrickhueller.com.

CPSIA information can be obtained
at www.ICGtesting.com
Printed in the USA
LVHW090202110220
646429LV00006BA/693